CONTAMINATION

BOOK SEVEN: RESISTANCE

BY. T.W. PIPERBROOK

ABOUT CONTAMINATION 7:RESISTANCE

The only way to survive is to resist...

After freeing Dan and Quinn, Sandy Duncan must fight to escape the lumberyard, while protecting the others she came to save. The infected lurk outside the gates.

Is her fate outside the lumberyard even worse than what she faces if she stays?

**Want to know the instant a
new release comes out?
Sign up for NEW RELEASE ALERTS
at: http://eepurl.com/qy_SH**

PREFACE

At the end of Contamination 6, I mentioned that there would be several standalone novels in the same world. The first of these was *Contamination: Dead Instinct.*

I decided to call this novel *Contamination 7* (as opposed to a standalone title), as it follows the story of Sandy and Reginald, both of whom were introduced in Book Four. I think it makes the most sense for readers to have read the rest of the series before this book.

The book picks up almost immediately after we left Sandy, so you'll see a brief cameo appearance by Dan and Quinn, whose story concluded in Book Six.

I hope you enjoy this return to the characters and the world of *Contamination.* I know I did!

Happy reading!
Tyler Piperbrook
June, 2016

BOOK FOUR RECAP

While trying to escape St. Matthews, Dan and Quinn rescue a girl named Sandy from the roof of a bank. Afterward, Reginald Morris, a criminal scavenging for supplies in town, steals Dan's station wagon.

Sandy tells Dan and Quinn she's been staying with Reginald and some others at the lumberyard, but that she was unaware of Reginald's criminal past. Unwilling to lose his uncontaminated food and supplies, Dan heads to the lumberyard in pursuit of his vehicle.

When they arrive, a young man named Charlie, who is guarding the gate, agrees to bring them in. Paranoid, or perhaps unstable, Reginald shoots Charlie, entraps and ties up Dan and Quinn, and interrogates them.

While the others are arguing, Sandy frees Dan and Quinn and leads them to their station wagon. She tells them to escape while she stays behind to help the others.

PART ONE
TWO SIDES

WHAT HAVE I DONE?

Sandy looked over her shoulder, catching a last glimpse of the station wagon that hung in the shadows. Dan and Quinn were huddled inside. In just a few minutes, the police officer and his daughter would drive off, leaving Sandy to face Reginald. Or at least, that was the plan.

She'd freed them and told them to leave. Sandy couldn't abandon the rest of the people in the lumberyard.

Hector, Marcia, Anabel, and Finn needed her help.

Doubt clawed at her mind like a rabid animal. What if she'd made a mistake? What if she'd done the exact thing that would get her killed? Heaving frantic breaths, Sandy rounded the corner of the warehouse, leaving the vehicle behind. Her hope was that she could get back inside the building quickly and avoid implication.

She slid her hand along the wall, looking for the exit door in the pale moonlight. She found it halfway down. Twisting the doorknob, she sucked in a breath and snuck back inside. Loud, angry voices told her the others were still arguing about Dan's fate. Reginald was the loudest. What Reginald didn't realize was that Sandy had already made the decision for him.

She moved through a dark office, listening for Dan and Quinn's car. Nothing. Had Reginald done something to it? Had he disabled the vehicle somehow?

She didn't see how, or when, but it was possible.

At least no one was guarding the gate outside. Everyone must be inside, arguing. She weaved between several desks and office chairs, following the glow of the lantern light that splashed over the main warehouse in the adjacent room. Through a dusty, dirt-streaked window, she saw Hector waving his hands at Reginald. Hector was a middle-aged, Hispanic man with a round frame. His hair was dark and thinning. His arguments to save Dan didn't appear to be getting through. Behind Hector were his family—his wife Marcia and his six-year-old daughter Anabel. A young man named Finn stood next to them.

Reginald's hand fell to his holstered pistol, malice in his eyes. Behind him were Billy, Simon, and Tom—a group of men that had been interrogating Dan and Quinn. Although they'd expressed doubt in killing Dan earlier, they appeared to have been swayed by the promise of safe food and water.

Using the commotion to her advantage, Sandy slipped back into the main warehouse, avoiding everyone's eyes. Her fear was that some clue on her face might give away what she'd done. Hector's and Reginald's' voices echoed off the cavernous ceiling. She breathed a sigh of relief, realizing the others were too preoccupied to notice her.

"Dan's lying!" Reginald spat, stepping closer to Hector. "We need to take care of him! He's involved in what's happening."

"How can we be sure?" Hector asked.

"I *know* he's in on it." Reginald pursed his lips emphatically. "No one could have all the information he does and not be involved. If you believe him, he's one of the only ones who survived in St. Matthews. And he's the only one with safe food and water. Isn't that proof enough?"

"I want to talk to him," Hector said plaintively. "I want to find out for myself."

"He's dangerous. He and his daughter need to go," Billy agreed from beside Reginald.

Hector fell silent for a moment. He looked over at Simon and Tom. "What do you think? Do you agree with this?"

The men traded an anxious glance and nodded.

Hector turned back to face Marcia, whose eyes glistened with tears. She shook her head no. Anabel was crying and holding onto her. Hector put his head in his hands. "I don't know how we're even considering this. You're talking about killing a police officer. I won't have any part in harming them. When this is over, I'll have to live with myself. Can you do the same?"

Reginald took a bold step toward Hector. "If you don't agree, you and your family can leave. The food stays here."

Sandy's eyes roamed between Reginald, Simon, Billy, and Tom. She wanted to step in, but she feared her intrusion might escalate the situation.

"So you're going to starve us?" Hector repeated.

Reginald's face reddened under the glow of the lanterns. It looked like he was sweating. "You haven't been out there recently," he shouted. "You don't know what it's like!"

"I know exactly what it's like," Hector tried, motioning to his family. "We survived and got here from New Mexico. Remember?"

"But you haven't done shit since. All you've done is keep guard. You haven't even gone on any supply runs. You don't deserve the food and water I found in that station wagon." Reginald cracked his neck. His eyes were wild and nervous; it was obvious the new world had cracked his already-violent mind. Or maybe something else was going on. His body was shaking.

Hector held up his hands. "With the rest of the food contaminated, we'll have nothing to eat. You're threatening us with infection, probably death."

Reginald reached for his gun. "Come any closer, and I'll do worse than that."

Fear crossed Hector's face. Reginald stared at him with the expression of a man past his threats.

Before anything could happen, Sandy stepped in and held up her hands. "Stop! We don't need to argue like this."

Reginald broke his combative stare and turned to face her. She kept stoic, even though she wanted nothing more than to disappear, or run from the room.

"There's no need to argue," she continued. "The only reason we're alive is because we've worked together. We need to cooperate."

Reginald blew an explosive breath. "You changed that by bringing Dan and Quinn here. This is your fault! You could've gotten all of us killed!"

"I didn't mean any harm by it. I was trying to help them, like they helped me in town."

Reginald's eyes narrowed as he took a step toward her. It seemed like he'd already forgotten about Hector and had focused his rage on her.

"Reginald, please, leave her alone," Hector said.

Sandy held up her hands to defend herself. Before she could finish her sentence, a car engine started outside. Everyone's attention turned to the windows, where headlights illuminated the pane. Tires crunched furiously as a car shot by, spitting up gravel, kicking up dust.

"What the hell?" Reginald shouted.

Dan and Quinn! Sandy thought.

2

EGINALD, SIMON, TOM, AND BILLY drew their guns and raced for the door, opening it in time to see a car battering through the gate.

"Goddamit!" Reginald screamed in rage.

The armed men raced into the parking lot. Gunshots split the air. The people left in the warehouse looked around frantically. Reginald's men had the only guns. It was an unlucky coincidence. *Or a planned one,* Sandy thought. She looked over at Hector, who had a knife tucked in his belt. She had one, also, from freeing Dan and Quinn. The others had small blades. Anabel buried her face in Marcia's shirt. Finn held up his hands, as if he might stop a bullet.

"We need to get out of here!" Sandy told them.

Hector nodded, fear in his eyes. Before they could determine a plan, Reginald raced back in the room. Simon was right behind him.

"Don't let them out of your sight! I don't trust them!" Reginald yelled.

Simon waved his pistol, eliciting gasps of fear from the people in the room. And then Reginald ran back outside. A few more bullets sounded from outside; moments later, a second car shot past the warehouse. Clouds of dust blew through the open doorway, creating a murky blackness.

And then both vehicles were gone and the warehouse was silent.

Sandy watched Simon. Her hope was that he wouldn't figure out what she'd done until she could figure out a way to get these people to safety.

She sized up Simon. He was in good shape — his arms were toned and tanned underneath his white muscle shirt. One of his arms had a full sleeve of tattoos. She'd gone on several supply runs with him, discussing lost family and sharing hopes of rescue, but those conversations seemed to have been forgotten in Reginald's spreading paranoia.

"Hand over your weapons!" Simon demanded.

Sandy watched him for a second, defiance flickering in her eyes before she reluctantly dug into her jeans. She pulled out her knife, dropping it in the dirt.

"The rest of you, too!" Simon ordered, waving his gun.

Hector relinquished his knife. The others dropped their small blades in the dirt and held up empty hands. Simon bent down and retrieved the weapons, then patted them down. When he was satisfied they were unarmed, he stepped back, trading his attention between them and the doorway. There was no sign of Reginald and his men, no sign of Dan and Quinn. The roar of car engines had segued to the sound of night insects.

Simon walked to the doorway, peered out into the night, and said, "The gate's open. Shit." He took a few steps into the parking lot, torn between guarding the people he'd been told to watch and shutting it. Finally, he seemed to make a decision. "Come with me."

He waved his pistol, herding the people in the warehouse in front of him. Sandy walked single-file with her scared companions as they entered the parking lot. The smell of burned tires was a stinging reminder that Dan and Quinn had escaped, while Sandy and the others were left behind.

"If you don't trust us, why not let us leave, like Reginald said?" Hector asked Simon.

"Be quiet." Simon's face grew hard. "We don't know how many creatures we might've stirred up with all the noise."

He flicked on a flashlight, illuminating the dusty parking lot and instructing them to hurry. Sandy swallowed and covered her mouth as she walked over the gravel, trying not to choke on dust, following the thin beam of Simon's flashlight. Between the dust and the darkness, she could barely see; every shadow resembled a creature, hissing and waiting to pounce.

The front gates were broken open where Dan had crashed through them. Simon swiveled his flashlight until he found the lock and chains in the gravel. Then he shone the beam on Sandy and the others, waving them over to the fence.

"We can help you," Sandy started. "You don't have to do this."

"Keep quiet, I said."

Simon scooped up the chains and lock and dug for the keys to the lock, keeping a wary eye on them. Sandy had the frantic thought that they should run through the gates, but they were more likely to get shot than get away. She looked over at Hector, who was holding Marcia and Anabel close. Finn watched her with a hopeless expression.

While Simon was busy with the gate, Marcia hissed at Sandy, "I saw you slipping out before. What were you doing?"

A feeling of panic washed over Sandy. She didn't think anyone had noticed. Taking a chance, she admitted, "I cut Dan and Quinn loose."

"My God," Hector said, mouth agape.

"Reginald will kill you!" Marcia whispered.

Sandy looked over at Simon, who was still securing the gates. "He'll kill all of us, if we don't get out of here. You heard his threats. You've seen what he's done. Something's wrong with him. We need to leave. If we don't, we'll die."

The others looked around nervously. Before they could concoct a plan, Simon swung the gates closed and locked them in. Sandy watched the entrance with the sinking feeling that none of them would ever see the other side of it again.

3

S ANDY LOOKED OVER HER SHOULDER, praying she wouldn't see headlights past the fence. Reginald would be back soon, with or without Dan and Quinn. And when he returned, their chances at escape would be slim.

She needed to figure something out. Fast.

With no choice but to walk quietly ahead of Simon, Sandy and the others entered the warehouse, surveying the shelves full of lumber and supplies. In the time Sandy had been staying here, she'd gotten used to the smell of wood and the odor of grease and equipment. Those scents were familiar enough to feel a little like home. But not anymore. Now the lumberyard was a place from which they needed to escape.

Simon closed the door and stationed himself in front of it, pointing his pistol at them. He instructed them to stand ten feet away. Mind brimming with desperate thoughts, Sandy attempted to rationalize with him.

"This is about food," Sandy guessed.

Simon remained quiet.

"You're afraid Reginald will starve you, just like he threatened to do to Hector and his family," Sandy said.

Simon looked away.

"Reginald killed Charlie. What makes you think he won't kill the rest of us?"

"Charlie's death was an accident," Simon argued, but without Reginald around, he didn't sound as convinced.

"He's persuaded every one of that. But it's not true. I was there."

Simon chewed his lip. "So was I. Reginald's been fair with me," he said. "He's the one who found the lumberyard. He's the one who's kept us safe this long."

"But he's turned against Hector and his family, and now he's turned against me. He'll do the same to you, as soon as you do something he doesn't like."

"I'll take that up with him when the time comes."

Realizing that her words weren't having an effect, Sandy struggled to think of another argument. Anabel cried, holding Marcia tightly, peering out from the folds of her mother's shirt.

"Listen, Simon," Hector tried again, taking a slow step toward him. "There's no reason to hold us here. Let us leave, like Reginald said. We won't come back."

"Quiet," Simon warned.

"There will be fewer mouths to feed without us," Hector pleaded. "You'll have a better chance at survival if we're not here."

Simon pointed his pistol directly at Hector's

chest. "I'm not doing a thing until Reginald's back."

"What if he dies? What if he doesn't come back?" Sandy asked.

Simon turned toward her. A curious expression crossed his face, and Sandy took a guess as to what that might mean. "You know where the supplies are."

"No, I don't."

"You do," Sandy said again. "I can tell by your expression."

Simon pursed his lips, but didn't say anything.

"This might be the chance we need to escape, Simon. If we take those supplies and leave, we might be able to find help. There has to be someone else out there—the military, the National Guard. We've talked about it on our supply runs. I know you've lost your sister. I lost my brother. We've all been through enough, Simon. We deserve to live."

"I don't believe anyone's out there anymore." Simon's face grew sad as he said the words. "The only thing I know for sure is what's here. And that's why I'm staying."

"For how long? Until Reginald decides he doesn't want to feed you anymore?"

Simon bit his lip as he grew angry. "He won't starve me," he said, but his eyes harbored doubts.

"He might, if he has to decide between feeding you and feeding himself. Reginald stole Dan's station wagon and left me to die while we were in St. Matthews. He has no allegiance to anyone. He's a convict, Simon."

"We've all done things," Simon said, waving his hand dismissively.

Sandy noticed Simon's eyes looked darker than she remembered. She realized she didn't know him well. He'd told her that he was a construction worker from Tucson, and that he'd escaped the creatures and made his way to St. Matthews after losing his sister. Regardless of what he might be hiding, the immediate threat was that she'd see headlights coming back toward the lumberyard. If Reginald returned, their hopes would be crushed.

"The food is just a temporary fix," she argued. "We'll need more of it. Whatever we have here won't last more than a few weeks."

"How will we find more?" Simon asked, the gun wavering in his hands.

Sensing she was getting through to him, Sandy persisted, "We can take the food and water, and we can look for help. We'll have a better chance at surviving together than staying with Reginald."

Simon opened and closed his mouth as he thought of an answer. Instead of replying, he looked over his shoulder, as if Reginald might be listening and waiting to accuse him.

"You can blame me if something happens," Hector said, stepping forward. "I have nothing left to lose."

Simon looked from one of them to the other. His eyes lingered on Anabel, who shielded her face while staying next to her mother. Finally, he lowered his gun and pointed at the shelves of lumber on the far side of the warehouse.

"I saw where Reginald hid the supplies. If we're going to take them, we better hurry."

4

"R EGINALD DIDN'T THINK I SAW where he put them, but I did," Simon explained as he hurried to a far corner of the warehouse. He threw a panicked look over his shoulder, as if Reginald might come charging through the door. He stopped and motioned toward a shelf about ten feet off the ground, holding up a lantern, illuminating stacks of wood.

"We should probably guard the door," he said.

"Finn, will you watch for Reginald's car?" Sandy called. "Let us know if you see headlights."

"Will do."

Finn ran across the warehouse and toward the entrance. He cracked the door and peered through. Simon moved a stepladder with wheels to the shelf.

"I'll climb," Sandy suggested. "I'm smaller, so I can move faster."

Simon nodded reluctantly, holding his gun at waist-level. "Okay."

He watched Sandy climb to the top of the ladder. She put her leg onto the shelf, straining, and pulled herself up and onto a stack of wood. The wood shifted as two boards clanked together, sending an echo through the warehouse.

"Crap," she swore.

"All the way back, you'll see several garbage bags," Simon called up.

Sandy scooted forward, using her hands to guide her. The shadowy light of the lantern barely lit the shelf on which she was crawling. For a moment, she envisioned creatures emerging from the wall and dragging her into the recesses of the warehouse, consuming her. Hot sweat poured down her face as she crawled across the boards. And then her hands were on the bags, and she was scooting back to the edge of the shelf and passing one down.

"Here you go!" she said to Simon.

He climbed up to meet her. They repeated the process several more times, until four bags of food sat on the warehouse floor.

"Last one," Sandy said, scooting in and retrieving another.

She paused before handing it down. A sting of guilt hit her. By taking all the supplies, she'd effectively be condemning Reginald, Billy, and Tom to death if the theory that they were immune wasn't true. But wasn't that the same fate with which Reginald threatened all of them?

Sucking in a breath, she passed the bag down to Simon.

A scream ripped their attention across the warehouse. Finn stumbled back through the doorway, flailing his arms. One of the creatures was latched onto him. He fell to the ground as the creature tore away a mouthful of his neck, hissing and groaning. Panic and confusion hit Sandy as she tried to figure out what was happening.

"Finn!" she screamed, scooting from her perch on the shelf.

Hector, Marcia, Anabel, and Simon were already racing for him. Sandy rushed down the ladder. Finn's screams of agony pierced through the warehouse. His hands flailed wildly at his sides as he tried to get out from underneath the thing that was pinning him down. Sandy ran across the warehouse, feeling powerless and too far away. Hector and Marcia reached Finn first, tugging at the creature's arms, but the creature was latched onto Finn, its long, dark hair swinging back and forth over its face as it attacked. Sandy couldn't even tell if it was male or female.

"Stay back!" Simon shouted, reaching the scene and aiming his pistol. He shot the creature in the head, sending it sprawling face first on top of Finn. The others reached in and pulled it off.

But it was too late.

Finn spat mouthfuls of blood and grabbed his neck.

"Jesus!" Sandy screamed as she took his side.

Finn groped blindly, as if someone, or something, might help him.

Another hiss drew their attention to the doorway. A creature ran at them from the parking lot. Hector slammed the door, but not in time. The hungry, writhing thing wedged itself in the frame, fighting and scratching. Sandy joined Hector, jumping to her feet and ramming the door with her shoulder, hoping to knock the thing back into the parking lot. The creature shrieked rabidly. Suddenly, it snaked an arm around the door and grabbed hold of Hector.

"Hector!" Sandy shrieked.

She tried to pry it off, but the creature had a firm grip.

An enraged yell sounded from behind them. Sandy turned. Simon rushed at the creature with Hector's knife. He stabbed the creature in the arm. All at once the creature recoiled, giving them enough room to slam the door closed. Hector bolted the door with a click.

"Thanks," Hector told Simon, panting for breath.

Simon nodded. The room went a decibel quieter. Outside, the groans of several other creatures echoed from the parking lot.

"How the hell are they getting in?" Simon asked in confusion.

"They must've slipped in before we got the gate closed," Sandy guessed, gasping. "Either that, or they found another way."

"All the commotion probably drew all of them from the area," Simon said. "We need to get out of here before it gets worse, if they haven't overrun the place already."

Anabel let out a frightened sob as she knelt next to Finn's body. In the frenzy of the attack,

Sandy had momentarily been distracted. She looked back at her companion, but Finn had gone lifeless. His eyes were eerily vacant, as if he'd died hours ago instead of seconds. Sandy wrung her hands, wishing there was a way to revive the lifeless young man, even though he was beyond saving. She exchanged a desperate glance with Hector.

"I found some towels!" Marcia said, appearing from behind them a beat too late.

She dropped them as she realized there was no bringing him back. Sandy bent down next to Finn's motionless body, a wave of guilt crashing over her. This was her fault. She'd told Finn to keep guard. But how could she have known? She wiped tears from her eyes.

A crash drew her attention back to the door. The door shook violently as more creatures threw themselves against it. Sandy pictured the things bashing their faces and bodies apart, willing to obliterate the last remnants of their humanity to procure a meal.

"We have to get out of here," she said.

"Did you see how many of them were out there?" Simon asked, watching the door.

"I'm not sure, but Reginald will be back soon," Hector said. "And then we'll have even more trouble. We should see if we can make it to the truck."

Sandy looked between Finn and the bags of supplies across the warehouse, listening to the cries of the creatures outside. Finn's death couldn't be for nothing. They needed to get out of the lumberyard.

"Maybe only a few got in," Simon said with a shrug.

Sandy nodded, hoping to God he was right.

5

THE CREATURES POUNDED THE WAREHOUSE door as Sandy, Simon, Hector, Marcia, and Anabel ran toward the office. Sandy fought the grief in her stomach. Finn shouldn't have died like that. But there was no time to mourn him now. They picked up the bags of food and water and ran into the next room, weaving around desks and chairs. When they reached the side door, they huddled next to it and regrouped.

"The pickup is past the next building," Simon whispered. "We'll have to go through the alley, into the parking lot to get to it. We won't be able to fit by the fence in back."

Sandy nodded, knowing that was true.

"Here," Simon hissed, handing her something in the dark.

Sandy reached out and felt her knife. She took it appreciatively. He handed the blades back to the others. She still didn't trust Simon, but he'd redeemed himself by saving Hector, and she didn't have time to question his loyalty.

A few errant shrieks pierced the lumberyard, but none seemed close.

"I'll go first," Simon whispered, opening the door and leading with his gun.

Before anyone could respond, he snapped on his flashlight and crept into the alley. His body was little more than a silhouette as he took a few steps, casting light on the ground, giving just enough visibility to guide them. Gathering courage, Sandy and the others followed. They moved as a terrified unit, muffling the sound of the bags in their arms. Sandy snuck quietly over the gravel. The alley felt like it extended for miles, even though it was only a hundred feet.

Reaching the end, Sandy stared into the dusty parking lot as the shrieks grew louder. Some of the creatures were inside the fence, but she guessed more were outside of it, as well. Plenty of them would come. They always did. Sandy kept her eyes on Simon's flashlight, hurrying after him.

A creature jumped from the blackness.

Simon cried out and raised his pistol, shooting it, sending it sprawling back into the dark. Marcia screamed as another creature emerged from the dust, latching onto Hector. Hector cried out and pushed it off, sending it tumbling to the ground. He knelt down and speared it with his knife.

Sandy looked around frantically. Before she could catch her bearings, another creature was scrabbling for her, arms outstretched. She raised her hands, dropped her bag, and met it with her knife, fending off its snapping teeth. Panic fought with survival instinct as the world became a vicious, biting mass and the creature overtook her. She smelled the dank odor of blood, sweat, and whoever had last fallen victim to it. Sandy tried stabbing, but the thing twisted one of Sandy's fingers. She cried out and kicked it in the leg, freeing herself, leaping backwards.

With a scream, she ran at it and sank her knife into its forehead. She pulled out the blade. The creature's eyes rolled back in its head and it fell.

Sandy breathed and stepped back.

"Are you okay?" Simon asked.

"I'm fine!" Sandy hissed, collecting her bag. "Let's go!"

They raced through the parking lot and past the next building. The windows were dark and dirt-streaked, harboring who knew what manner of danger. Hector cursed as he tripped on a pile of loose stones. Marcia and Anabel ran next to him. Sandy clutched her knife and her bag. Hisses drifted from the blackness, as if the creatures were surrounding them in all directions. It was impossible to tell how many, or where they were.

Rounding the corner of the building, they came upon the white pickup. Simon shone the flashlight, searching for the door handle. He dug in his pocket for the keys.

"Get in!" he yelled, as he opened the door.

He jumped into the driver's seat while Hector and his family tumbled into the back. Sandy raced for the passenger's side. Dirty exhaust plumed into the air as Simon started the engine. The truck's interior lights illuminated his hardened face.

"Drive!" Sandy shouted as she got in.

Simon clutched the wheel. He reached for the shifter.

Before he could drive, the driver's side window shattered.

Glass sprayed the interior. Reaching hands groped for Simon. He craned his head away from the window, stomping the gas, but the truck was still in park.

"Dammit!" he shouted.

He grunted as the pistol was knocked from his hands. Sandy reached frantically for the shifter. She found reverse. The tires squealed as the vehicle careened backward. Sandy felt a jolt as they ran over something, and then they were backing wildly through the parking lot.

Sandy's stomach plummeted as one of the creatures tore at the passenger's side mirror. Simon reclaimed the wheel, but not in time.

"Look out!" Sandy screamed.

The rear of the truck collided with one of the lumberyard buildings. Sandy's head snapped forward and she threw her arms in front of her, protecting her face. She flew back in her seat as the vehicle stopped. She sat in stunned silence while she caught her breath, listening to the moans of the oncoming creatures. Her body ached from the impact, but nothing seemed broken. At least, she didn't think so. She looked over her shoulder, surveying the people in the backseat. Everyone was fine, except Hector, who had suffered a bloody gash in his forehead.

"Hector!" Marcia exclaimed.

The tires spun and stopped, spun and stopped. Sandy listened to the purr of the engine and the snarls of running creatures that were quickly catching up.

"Get out of here, Simon!" she shrieked.

The backseat came alive as Marcia and Anabel screamed similar things. Simon hit the gas. The vehicle groaned in protest as it unglued from the building.

The pickup flew forward.

Several creatures emerged from the darkness, throwing their bodies at the vehicle and bouncing off the side. The headlights illuminated several snarling, vicious faces. The creatures' eyes were jet-black.

Simon steered toward the gate, which was already open.

The creatures had knocked it down.

Sandy winced as a creature glanced off the front bumper. One ran straight for Simon's window, but he turned the wheel and clipped it with the front of the truck, sending the creature reeling back with a screech. They plowed through several more bodies, each one causing enough impact to convince Sandy they were going to stall or stop.

But they didn't. They kept going.

Soon, they were driving through the gates. And then they were away from the lumberyard, careening into the night.

6

R EGINALD'S BLOOD RACED AS HE gripped the steering wheel of the Buick. He stared into the dusty road as a few creatures emerged from the road's shoulder, roused by the noise of the car's engine. He could no longer see Dan's station wagon. The fucker had gotten enough of a jump to lose him.

"Hopefully none of those things will show up at the lumberyard," Billy said.

"Let someone else worry about it," Reginald snarled, his eyes flitting back and forth across the road.

He felt a shiver up his arms as the meth he'd shot up coursed through his veins. His pulse was beating so fast he could feel it behind his eyeballs. He had a stockpile in the lumberyard, several boxes he'd tucked away in one of the furthest shacks. He didn't think anyone knew about it.

That was the first thing he'd done when the shit hit the fan.

Get to the dealer...

Find the stash...

The motherfucker had already been dead, his face chewed off by one of the creatures.

That meant the stuff was Reginald's. It hadn't

gone easily, though. Several others had had the same idea as Reginald. No sooner had he discovered the dealer's hiding place than he'd been interrupted. Two people had come into the room, yelling and screaming. Reginald had pounded their faces in with the first thing he'd come across — a baseball bat. He barely remembered what they looked like, because the celebration that had ensued afterward had been enough to forget about what he'd done.

Reginald smiled. He'd do the same thing to Dan, once he caught him.

Anger overtook Reginald. He wanted nothing more than to find Dan and pay him back for everything he'd been through. Not only for escaping the lumberyard, but also for the things he'd done prior to the end of the world.

It'd been a year since Reginald had been released from jail. In the past decade, he'd wasted several years of his life in a cage, all because of Dan Lowery. Dan had first arrested him in 2008 for car theft, and he'd shown him no sympathy. Neither had the judge, who had given Reginald a strict probation that he'd unwittingly violated, landing him in jail.

To be fair, Reginald had learned a lot while in prison. He'd learned how to fight, how to steal, and how to survive a beating.

He wanted to share those lessons with Dan.

He'd kill Dan Lowery when he found him, and he'd make his daughter watch.

White commercial buildings lined either side

of the road, illuminated for brief seconds by the Buick's headlights. Reginald, Billy, and Tom checked the cross streets, parking lots, and main thoroughfare for signs of Dan. Reginald wasn't sure how Dan and Quinn had escaped, but it didn't much matter anymore. Dan's escape was further proof of his guilt. That would give Reginald the excuse to kill him, no matter what the others said.

The meth running through his body was like a jolt of energy, revving him up and making him see more clearly than anyone else around him. Reginald wiped his nose.

"Reginald, watch out!" Billy shouted.

Reginald swerved around a creature that had stumbled into the road, black eyes flashing. He cried out and straightened the car, increasing speed.

7

SANDY GASPED FOR BREATH AS she looked behind them at the lumberyard, watching it disappear into the blackness. Wind whipped through the broken driver's side window, reminding her of the hands that had been reaching for Simon just moments earlier.

At least we got away.

Hector groaned in the backseat.

"Hector, are you all right?" Sandy asked, turning her attention to the injured man.

"I-I think so," Hector called over the wind. He ran his fingers over the gash in his forehead, smearing blood down his face. His eyes were wide and confused.

"My God, Hector," Marcia said, shaking her head with concern.

Sandy reached up and turned on the overhead light. Hector looked between Sandy and the others. His face was a twisted mask of pain.

"I hit my head right there," Hector explained, pointing at the back of Simon's seat. Blood stained the metal bars below the headrest. "I didn't have time to brace myself."

"We need to stop the bleeding," Marcia said, looking around.

Sandy dug through the glove compartment, searching for something with which to assist him. She found a few napkins tucked between some registration papers and handed them back to Marcia. Marcia held them against the wound. Sandy looked at Simon. He drove in grim silence, watching the road.

Sandy checked herself over. She was unharmed, except for some aches and a splitting headache from being jolted around during the collision.

Maybe it was the horror of what her life had become.

Ever since the start of the contamination, her life had been a flurry of running, fighting, and surviving, doing things she'd never thought she'd have to do.

A week ago, she'd been living in an apartment with her brother, Ben. On the day the world ended, she'd come home after her shift, finding him in the hallway of their apartment complex feasting on another tenant. He'd been infected. He'd chased her down the hallway. Frantic, she'd raced into their apartment, barely dodging his groping hands as he'd crashed through the door behind her. In a last, desperate attempt to get away, she'd locked herself in the bathroom, but he'd slammed against the door until he'd burst in.

If it weren't for the hair dryer she'd left on the sink, Ben would've killed her. Sandy shuddered as she pictured what she'd done to her brother. His dented, bloodied face still haunted her nightmares. Ben had been her older brother, the one she'd turned to when life's problems were too much.

And now Ben was dead.

When Sandy was twelve, Sandy and Ben's parents had died in a car accident. The loss had devastated both of them. She'd considered dropping out of school, but Ben had pulled her out of her depression, convincing her to keep going. He'd supported her dreams, helped her pull her life together, and persuaded her to finish high school and college. After she'd graduated, he'd encouraged her to pursue her passion of becoming a hairdresser. She'd finished her training and obtained a job at a local salon in St. Matthews. Her goal was to one day own her own shop.

And now that goal was gone, and Ben was no longer there to encourage her.

Sandy pushed back the painful memory that Finn's death had conjured. She didn't have time for it right now. She needed to help the people in the truck. In the preceding days, she'd found ways to survive, scrounging for supplies in St. Matthews, hiding, avoiding the creatures. She hoped she could do the same thing now.

She tried to convince herself Ben would be proud of her.

"I don't know where I'm going," Simon said, interrupting her thoughts.

"You're from Tucson," Sandy recalled.

"Yeah, I'm not too familiar with St. Matthews."

"Stay on 4th North."

She surveyed the dark road ahead as Simon shook the broken glass from his lap with his pistol.

Sandy asked, "Do you have any spare ammunition?"

"A few magazines," Simon said, patting his pants. "Reginald, Billy, and Tom took the rest."

Looking up the road, she pointed to a passing sign. "When we get to the intersection, take a left. We can decide what to do from there."

Simon nodded.

Sandy turned off the overhead light and looked behind them again. She half-expected to see a pair of headlights following them, weaving back and forth over the road. But the road was empty. Where were Reginald, Billy, and Tom? She hoped that Dan and Quinn had gotten away.

Dan's a police officer. He should be safe.

Sandy told herself that, even though she wasn't sure. She had enough to worry about. At least she'd gotten the others out of the lumberyard.

She turned her attention to the people in the backseat. Hector's eyes fluttered open and closed. It looked like he was fighting for consciousness.

"I think I've stopped the bleeding," Marcia explained. "But he's in pain."

"I hope he doesn't have a concussion," Sandy said.

"How would we be able to tell?" Marcia asked.

"I had a bicycling accident when I was a kid. My parents kept me awake for twenty-four hours so they could watch me," Sandy explained. "I don't know much else, but I remember that. It's probably a good idea to keep him alert."

Worry creased Marcia's brow as she nodded. "Stay with us, Hector. Don't close your eyes. Okay?"

Sandy wished they had a place to lie him down, or keep better watch over him. One thing was certain: stopping wouldn't be smart.

"There's the turn," Sandy said, pointing it out to Simon as he took it. "If we stay straight, we'll hit the downtown area. I doubt we want to go that way. Our best bet is to head away from St. Matthews."

"Over the mountains?" Simon asked, pointing in the distance.

"Maybe," Sandy said. She watched him. "How much gas do we have?"

Simon read the fuel gauge. "We're almost empty."

Sandy swallowed. They'd been meaning to get more gas on the next trip to town. "We'll look for a place to stop," she called over the backseat to Marcia. "Maybe we'll find something to help Hector. But first we should get far away from the lumberyard."

The moon cast beams of light through the sparse trees around them as they kept driving. Small, one-story commercial buildings appeared on the roadside, their windows smashed by looters, creatures, or both. Sandy kept an eye on the mountains in the distance that served as a border around the town. She'd always loved the views in St. Matthews, but now the entire town felt foreign and strange, as if she'd warped into some nightmarish reality. She wondered whether she'd spend the rest of her days with the creatures a step behind.

What if Simon was right, and they were truly the last ones left?

Fleeting shadows ran through the trees. Every so often, a guttural screech emanated from the darkness. The broken driver's side window reinforced a feeling of danger. Sandy hoped they wouldn't run into Reginald on the road. The truck might as well be a bullhorn, echoing in the night. Anyone around would hear them.

"Do you think Reginald caught up with Dan and Quinn?" she asked Simon.

Simon shifted in his seat. He grimaced. "I hope not, for their sake."

Sandy watched Simon. What she wanted to say, but didn't dare, was that she still wasn't sure if she could trust him, either, after what he'd done at the lumberyard. But for now, she'd keep that to herself.

He's the only one with a gun.

8

REGINALD, BILLY, AND TOM HAD driven far enough from the lumberyard that the commercial area had segued to the center of town. Several times, Reginald turned down cross streets and tore through alleyways, certain he'd find the station wagon. Each time he was angered to find only bodies, cars, and wreckage.

"Maybe we should get back to the lumberyard," Tom suggested. "The cop and his daughter are probably already dead."

"They're not," Reginald snapped, unwilling to believe otherwise. "We'll find them."

"Our supplies are back there," Billy said, cranking a thumb over his shoulder.

"We're not turning around yet," Reginald said, wiping the sweat from his brow. "Maybe in a while, but not yet."

He watched the buildings around him, envisioning the station wagon in each parking lot. He crooked his head as he turned down a corner, certain he'd find what he was looking for.

Where was the station wagon?

At any moment it'd materialize. At any moment, it'd —

Reginald took a quick turn, screeching the

tires. The car jolted as he ran over a tipped garbage can. He looked in the rearview and saw it rolling away.

"Dammit."

"What are you doing?" Billy asked.

"I saw lights ahead," Reginald said, his mind spitting thoughts faster than he could process them. Or maybe he was just thinking more clearly than the others.

"Are you sure?" Billy asked, leaning forward and bracing his arms against the dashboard.

Reginald increased speed as the road straightened and the headlights revealed a slew of sideways automobiles. He weaved around them, narrowly missing them, looking for the twin beams he'd seen. Where was Dan? Was it someone else? Dark shapes flitted by the Buick as they passed a slew of telephone poles. He doubted someone else would be driving in the same area, at the same time. In the past few days, they hadn't seen many survivors.

He scrutinized every object, searching for the station wagon. His eyes were sharp and focused as he pushed the vehicle faster. Whoever it was, he'd catch up to them.

9

"I SEE A GAS STATION UP ahead," Sandy noted, pointing.

Simon tapped the brakes as they approached an eerily deserted parking lot. A dark, square building sat in the middle. The moon illuminated several shadowed gas pumps, the boxes and hoses resembling mythical creatures coiled in slumber. Sandy saw no cars, as if the employees had known what was coming and had closed down. The more likely scenario was that they'd gone for help and never found it.

"It looks deserted," Simon agreed.

"Maybe we can find fuel, or something for Hector," Sandy said. "But we better make it quick. It's not safe out here with Reginald driving around. Or with those things everywhere."

Simon hesitated a moment. "The power won't be on. We'll have to find a can."

Sandy nodded, familiar with the routine.

Simon pulled into the parking lot. The headlights illuminated the building's windows, revealing several broken ones. Other than that, there didn't appear to be much evidence of looting. Sandy looked around. The nearest buildings were a few hundred feet away. She didn't see any of the creatures. Maybe they'd have a stroke of luck and get in and out safely.

Simon pulled to a stop and let the car idle. He looked at Sandy.

"Are you coming?" he asked.

She hesitated, recalling how he'd held a gun on her. They'd gotten along fine on previous supply runs, but things had changed.

"I know you don't trust me. But if we don't get some gas and get away from here, Reginald will find us," Simon said.

She turned to the backseat and asked Marcia, "Will you be all right here?"

Marcia nodded. "Sure. Be careful."

Sandy didn't have to ask to know the double meaning behind that statement.

She swallowed and exited the vehicle.

Sandy crept alongside Simon as they walked toward the gas station. She clutched her knife in a sweaty hand. Looking back at the truck, she saw the silhouettes of Marcia, Hector, and Anabel, watching.

"I hope they'll be all right," Sandy whispered.

"They'll be fine. We just have to make it quick."

She followed Simon toward the gas station's entrance. He shone the light on the gas station's broken windows, revealing fractured glass and an interior filled with scattered merchandise.

She hoped the people who had raided the store were gone, and that they'd left behind something useful.

The front door was locked, but they found a broken window large enough to climb through.

Sandy quelled the sound of her footsteps on broken glass as she tiptoed inside. She immediately went to the door and unlocked it. That would be a safer way to escape. She listened for scuttling sounds warning them they weren't alone. The air was quiet and still. Sandy recalled a birthday she'd had when her parents had surprised her. They'd taken her out to the store, and when they'd gotten back, her family and friends had been ready to spring out and sing to her. Birthdays like that had ended after her parents had died.

Maybe if we hadn't moved from Chicago to St. Matthews, Ben would still be alive.

Sandy repressed the thought. For all she knew, Chicago was just as devastated as St. Matthews.

Having determined that the store was empty, Simon investigated a tipped shelf full of medicine, pointing it out to Sandy.

"Pain relievers," he whispered.

Sandy pocketed several bottles of ibuprofen. She also found some gauze and alcohol, and she carried them with her. Sandy and Simon searched the rest of the store, finding little they could use except another flashlight and some batteries. The food and drinks were tempting, but dangerous. Who knew what was contaminated?

"I don't see any gas cans in here," Simon hissed. "They've probably already been taken. Let's check the storage room."

Sandy nodded and followed. They walked over torn packages of food and scattered drinks until they reached an open door in the back that looked like it had been kicked down. The door hung on one hinge; the middle was dented with a mark the size of a man's boot.

Walking through, Sandy found herself in a backroom nearly the size of the store. A familiar, fetid odor reached her nose as she surveyed several rows of merchandise. Her heart beat faster as she looked for the source, but couldn't find it.

"Be careful," Simon warned.

She held her breath as they snuck down the first aisle, exploring the shelves and floor, looking for gasoline. On each shelf she saw only items they couldn't use: open soda cans, packages of food that had been ripped open by looters or brave, scavenging animals.

Walking ahead of Sandy, Simon led the way and shone the flashlight down the next aisle. An exclamation from him made her jump. She held up her knife. Sandy was certain she'd find a hissing, bloodthirsty creature. Instead she found Simon gaping at something.

"Jesus," he muttered, pointing at the end of the aisle.

In between two shelves full of food, a gas station attendant laid motionless, legs splayed out in front of him, his uniform shirt smeared in blood, his face half-chewed off. Sandy gagged. She'd seen plenty of bodies in similar conditions while in St. Matthews center, but it never dulled the shock.

"Looks like he was planning a getaway," Simon said.

He moved his light from the dead body to a tipped can of gasoline and a backpack stuffed with scavenged supplies. He reached for the gas can.

Most was spilled and puddled on the floor, but there was still some inside. Simon righted the container with caution, as if the already-rotting corpse might come alive and accuse him of stealing. Then he rifled through the bag, finding only toiletries and food they couldn't trust.

"I didn't see any cars outside."

"Me, neither. Maybe his vehicle was stolen."

"Either way, this gas can will do us more good than it'll do him."

Exiting the store, Sandy looked for the shadows of her companions in the truck's backseat. She was relieved to see Hector, Marcia, and Anabel craning their heads in anticipation of their return. She breathed an anxious sigh. The parking lot was as desolate as when they'd left it.

Simon used the gas can to replenish the truck

while Sandy stood next to him. A guttural cry in the distance made her tense. She looked around, but couldn't see the creature stalking them.

"We're lucky to have gotten in and out," Simon said. "Now let's get the hell out of here."

"OVER THERE!" BILLY CRIED TO Reginald. Reginald clenched the wheel as headlights appeared in the distance. He knew he hadn't been mistaken.

He watched a car swerve down a street in the distance, knocking aside debris and trying to get away. Dan was probably inside, and scared. *He should be.* Reginald stomped the gas, narrowly missing one of the infected. The creature stumbled backward and stared after them as it disappeared into the night.

Billy and Tom shifted nervously in their seats, aiming their rifles out the windows. Reaching the place where he'd last seen the vehicle, Reginald mimicked the vehicle's turn, throwing on his high beams. He didn't care if Dan knew he was coming.

Dan couldn't stop him now.

They entered a dense street filled with shops and two and three-story buildings. Reginald squinted as he determined their location. Having lived in St. Matthews most of his life, he was familiar with the roads, but the absence of power threw off his sense of direction. Old landmarks were covered up or destroyed. Rubbish and debris filled streets normally filled with people and traffic. He took several turns and narrowed the gap with the distant vehicle.

A few blocks away, several broken-down, abandoned vehicles cluttered the street. The other driver was forced to hit the brakes. After weaving in and out of a few of them, the street became impassable and the driver stopped.

"Here we go!" Reginald yelled to the others. "We got 'em!"

Reginald weaved dangerously around a downed bicycle and a broken television, blocking the other car. Bright taillights illuminated the trunk. Reginald frowned.

It wasn't a station wagon. It was a red sedan.

Had Dan and Quinn changed vehicles? He didn't see how, or when, but it was possible. Perhaps they meant to throw him off. Before Reginald could make sense of the situation, two people rushed from the vehicle in a crouch, heading into a nearby building. Reginald squinted, trying to make them out in the dark. He parked the Buick and threw open the door.

To Tom and Billy, he said, "Let's go!"

"It doesn't look like them!" Tom protested.

"Let's go!" Reginald repeated.

He jumped from the vehicle and surveyed the interior of the sedan. A warning bell announced the door was ajar. The interior lights blazed, revealing an empty vehicle. Reginald reached over and shut the door, silencing the annoying noise. He looked at the building. The people had run inside an old-fashioned restaurant with two stories, a front porch containing tipped, broken tables and chairs, and smashed windows.

Reginald stalked from the road to the porch, his men behind him. The front door hung on one hinge. From somewhere inside, footsteps clapped up a flight of stairs. Reginald moved at a crouch, pistol pointed, knowing better than to run into an ambush.

"Stay low and watch out," he warned Billy and Tom.

He looked around the debris-ridden street, verifying that none of the creatures were close by, then walked from the sidewalk to the porch, stepping around smashed plates and silverware. He signaled Billy and Tom to flank the front door.

The building's interior was pitch black. He heard people panting and running, then a crash as someone knocked into something. A panicked cry echoed through the building.

I've got them now.

If Dan and Quinn had weapons, they'd have warned him to stay back, not run in fear. Reginald smiled. He pulled a flashlight from his pants and flicked it on. He shone it inside the restaurant, revealing a large dining room that had probably once been eloquent, but was now trashed and littered with furniture. The air reeked of rotten food that had been prepared and left out to fester. Several bodies were sprawled on the floor, half-eaten and obviously dead. A balcony overlooked the enormous dining room, extending around the perimeter of the upper floor. He shone his light up at the railing, catching sight of a face.

"Upstairs!" he hissed.

The face disappeared and the footsteps continued.

Reginald's mirth turned to anger. Dan and Quinn had outwitted him; they'd gotten away. Not only had they escaped, but they were taunting him, leading him on a chase to avoid retribution. He let that anger drive him as he rushed into the building with Billy and Tom, angling his flashlight up the stairs. He snuck up them quietly, keeping low as he and his men hustled up to the second floor. Reginald had the advantage. Dan and Quinn were running in the dark, but he had a light, and he had them outgunned.

Reaching the second floor, Reginald hesitated. More tables and chairs were scattered everywhere. The railing was broken away in several places where people had fought with the creatures and failed. Reginald saw several open doorways along the outskirts of the floor. The footsteps had ceased. Wherever Dan and Quinn were hiding, he'd uncover them.

He'd check every goddamned room.

He moved to the first door, shone his light in, and motioned for Billy and Tom to aim their rifles. The room was filled with supplies—folded tablecloths and napkins on shelves. They moved on to a second doorway, looking into a small, secluded dining room with several chewed, decaying bodies. Nothing.

Reginald swung his pistol into the third room, a similar layout as the second, with knocked over furniture. A breeze kicked up from outside, blowing through the smashed out windows, kicking up curtains. There were no closets or doors. He saw nothing behind the tipped, battered furniture. He was about to leave when he spotted an overturned table in the corner. Unlike the rest of the room, this appeared to be purposefully positioned. Signaling Billy and Tom, Reginald shone his light on the table. Then he slowly backed away.

He took cover behind the doorway.

He hissed, "Got you now, you fuckers."

The room went artificially still.

Someone was here. He could feel it.

"Come out now, and I'll spare Quinn."

Reginald was lying, of course. He had no intention of keeping his word. He watched intently for movement, ready to fire at the first sign of a weapon. He'd prefer to take Dan alive, but he'd do what he had to. He was about to speak again when a man with dark hair stepped slowly from behind the table, holding up a broken table leg, surrendering. The man's eyes flitted nervously around the room as he watched the doorway. Reginald made the surprise determination that it wasn't Dan.

"Please," the man pleaded. "It's just my

girlfriend and I. We were looking for help. We saw someone chasing us."

A female voice echoed from behind the table. "Don't shoot! We don't mean any harm!"

A pulse of anger ran through Reginald. These people weren't Dan. They'd wasted his time. They'd distracted him enough that he'd lost whatever lead he had. He looked back at Billy and Tom, who watched him with confused expressions.

Reginald fired at the dark-haired man, catching him in the stomach. The man dropped to his knees, blood leaking from his gut as the broken table leg clattered to the floor. His lips quivered in surprise. He looked at Reginald with a combination of shock and terror, clasping his hands over the fresh wound. Reginald felt a strange feeling of elation.

He shone the light on the bleeding, begging man.

"Y-you shot me!" the man gurgled, as if Reginald might take back what he'd done.

Billy and Tom backed away from Reginald. They lowered their weapons, as if they might run away.

Reginald shot the man in the head. A sense of righteousness coursed through him as he watched the man crumple.

"Jesus!" Billy muttered.

Reginald stepped toward the table. A girl ran out from behind it, heading toward the far corner of the room. She screamed as she fled, dragging

T.W. Piperbrook

her hands along the wall, pleading for her life. She stumbled near the broken windows. Reginald followed her with his pistol, gritting his teeth, shining the flashlight in her eyes, blinding her. She held her hands in front of her face.

Before he could shoot, the girl lost her balance and toppled through the open window, landing at the base of the building with a thud. And then the night was silent again, except for the cool breeze blowing through the windows.

11

ANDY, SIMON, HECTOR, MARCIA, AND Anabel drove away from the gas station, watching several creatures emerge from the shadows. A few of them raced toward the truck, but Simon was easily able to outrun them. Soon they were far enough away to relax slightly.

Sandy gave Marcia the pain relievers and supplies they'd collected from the gas station. Marcia administered them to Hector, who used one of the bottled waters from the bags to swallow the pills.

After driving a few more miles, the scenery transitioned from a commercial area to an area of wide, open desert. Sandy realized she hadn't seen a building in a while. Night insects chittered around them. Sandy recalled drives she'd taken in the desert with Ben, taking in scenery, escaping the worries of the workweek. Those drives had always been accompanied with discussions of dreams, goals, and the things they missed about their childhood and their parents. Thinking about them now, Sandy had a twinge of nostalgia.

Times like that were much different than the silent, nervous drive she was taking now.

"Something's wrong," Simon said, looking at the dashboard.

"What is it?" Sandy asked.

"We're overheating."

Sandy snapped her attention to the temperature gauge, which shuddered above the top line. The engine light popped on. "Why is that happening?"

"We either damaged something or it's a mechanical issue," Simon said, pounding the wheel.

"Shit," Sandy said.

"What do we do?" Marcia asked worriedly from the backseat.

"Ideally, we fix it. But I don't have any tools. And I won't be able to see much at night. We'll have to at least wait until the engine cools off. Goddamnit," Simon cursed.

Sandy recalled the thumps she'd felt during their escape. Any one of them could've damaged the underside of the vehicle. Before she could speculate further, Simon pulled off the road and shut off the car. He pulled the flashlight from his pocket and reached for the door handle.

"I'll get out and take a look, even though I doubt I can do anything," he grunted.

Simon popped the hood, opened the door, and stepped out into the street with the gun. A moment later, she saw him shining his flashlight under the hood. She looked in the backseat. Hector, Marcia, and Anabel watched Sandy with frightened expressions.

"I still don't trust him," Marcia whispered to

Sandy. "If we hadn't talked sense into him, we would've still been at the lumberyard."

"If he betrayed us once, he might do it again," Hector said worriedly.

Sandy nodded. "I don't know what to think, either. Regardless, if we don't have a vehicle, we're going to have bigger problems than Simon. I'm going to get out and keep watch."

"I'll come with you," Hector said adamantly, starting to get up.

"No. You should rest."

Marcia reinforced Sandy's suggestion by holding Hector's arm.

"I'll be careful," Sandy persuaded them. "If I see any of those things around, I'll warn you."

She opened the door and stepped onto the side of the road. She surveyed the flat, vacant landscape. The moon illuminated patchy scrub brush. There were no buildings close by. To the north hung the White Mountains. Simon was focused on the engine. He creased his face as he jiggled some wires. Finally, he tucked his pistol in his pants and flashed his light at the undercarriage.

"I need to look underneath," he said. "Can you cover me?"

Simon watched her for a moment, as if he might not trust *her*, then hunched down and slid underneath the truck, shining the flashlight. Sandy held her knife, looking up and down the street, her heart beating fast and hard. They were broken down, stuck in this hellish nightmare together.

Regardless of what happened at the lumberyard, they had to find a way out.

Sandy looked up at the White Mountains.

She pursed her brow as she scrutinized a tall building in the distance, trying to determine exactly where they were. The darkness was disorienting. She was on the verge of recognition when Simon emerged from underneath the truck, his face grave in the orange glow of the flashlight.

"I think I found the problem," he said.

Sandy's heart fluttered. "What is it?"

"The oil pan has a hole. That explains why we're overheating." Simon returned to the engine and checked the dipstick. "Yep. The tank's dry."

"We can't drive, then?"

"We'll crack the head gasket if we do," Simon explained. "Besides, we won't get far with the truck in this condition. Our best bet is to find another vehicle."

Sandy looked up and down the road, but saw no other cars, abandoned or otherwise. From inside, she heard Marcia checking on Hector. Sandy was worried about him. She was worried about all of them. Her headache still blazed behind her eyes, and her body ached from the collision.

Refocusing on the building in the distance, she realized they were near the St. Matthews Elementary School.

"Do you know what that building is?" Simon asked.

"Yes. That's the St. Matthews Elementary School."

"Is that where you went to school?" Simon asked.

"No. I grew up in Chicago. I moved here a few years ago with my brother."

"That's right," Simon said, remembering. "Your brother died at the start of this. I'm sorry."

Sandy cleared her throat and pushed away the awful memory. "In any case, the elementary school might be a good place to hole up until morning. Since it's summertime, there might not have been anyone in the building."

"That sounds like a good plan."

"Can we drive there?"

"It's possible, but we'd risk ruining the only vehicle we have. We should wait a half hour until it cools off. But it'd probably be quicker to walk."

"Okay. I just hope Hector is up for it."

Hector groaned as they helped him out of the backseat. "I'll stop complaining now," he joked, but the expression on his face showed he was still in pain. "I'm just a little dizzy."

"Take it easy, Hector," Marcia said.

Sandy stared up the street, as if the elementary school might've disappeared. But it was there, looming in the distance, looking less like a school and more like some haunted attraction, waiting for some foolhardy people to come near it. She saw no cars or signs of life around it.

"We should take as much food as we can comfortably carry," Simon suggested. "We can hide the rest."

Simon and Sandy retrieved a few bags and carried them, hiding the remainder of the food and water under the seats. Marcia and Anabel helped Hector.

"Stay quiet," Simon said, turning his pistol in his hands.

They started up the road in a nervous group, leaving the truck behind. Sandy glanced back at the vacant vehicle. With each step, they were farther from a refuge. But the truck wasn't much of a refuge, anyway. With its missing window, the vehicle would only stave off the creatures for only a few moments.

We need better protection than that.

The humid air stuck to Sandy's skin, making her tank top feel sticky. She wiped away the sweat from her forehead. A deep quiet had settled over the moonlit road, amplifying the occasional scuff of their shoes and the intermittent screech of night animals. Hector seemed to be walking fine, though she heard him sucking in pained breaths every now and again. Marcia and Anabel stuck by his side. Sandy and Simon kept on either end of the group.

Sandy stared at the school in the distance, grateful they'd found it, but nervous about what they might find there. The desolate building might mean safety. But it also might mean that others had chosen the same location, and those people might be as ill-intentioned as Reginald.

Loud footsteps made her look over at her companions. She was about to warn them to be quiet when she realized it wasn't them.

Sandy grabbed Marcia's arm, forcing her and the others to a halt as the footsteps continued slapping the earth.

Getting closer.

Something was approaching from the side of the road.

Simon swiveled, aiming his gun. Sandy caught a glimpse of a figure sprinting through the desert shrubs in the moonlight. Its rabid snarls gave it away as one of the creatures. She saw a bare chest, a few scraps of clothing hanging from a weathered body. Marcia gasped and backpedaled with Hector and Anabel. Sandy dropped her bag of food and clutched her knife.

"I've got it!" she said.

"I'll shoot!" Simon said.

"No. You'll make too much noise," Sandy countered.

The creature ran in the direction of Hector and his family, but Sandy stepped in front of them, causing it to redirect its focus. Her heart pounded fiercely as the thing got close enough to smell. Without a word, she thrust her knife into the thing's face, listening to the slick sound of blade meeting flesh. She pulled the knife free, blood splattering her face. She grimaced and stepped back. The thing collapsed.

"Jesus, Sandy," Hector exclaimed.

More footsteps interrupted their relief.

Sandy looked in all directions. Another two creatures were running down the road, but Simon was ready with his pistol this time. There was no time to be quiet. He walked straight at them, creating a buffer from the group and firing. The first bullet went wide, ricocheting off the asphalt. The second connected. The first creature plummeted to the ground in a heap, emitting a last snarl and slapping the road. The second fell behind it as Simon shot it with a bullet in the head. The gunshots echoed through the street and off the distant mountains. Sandy exhaled as the desert fell quiet.

She wiped the blood from her cheeks, thankful that they'd survived.

"So much for staying undetected," Simon muttered.

"More will come from the commotion," Sandy said, recalling the lumberyard. "We need to get moving."

12

THEY MOVED DOWN THE ROAD at a faster pace. Even Hector seemed to have found a burst of strength, moving quietly and without complaint. Simon led the group while Sandy stuck alongside the others.

The distant building grew closer. Looking back, Sandy could no longer see the truck, as if night had swooped in and devoured it. They'd taken the keys, but Sandy found herself wondering if they'd ever return.

The future was as uncertain as it had been at the lumberyard with Reginald. Like everything else, the elementary school was a temporary destination.

The days of scrounging, hiding, and hoping were back.

Sandy recalled the times she'd spent huddled alone in buildings, thinking she was the last survivor, with only the screeches of hunting creatures to keep her company. Those had been the times she'd questioned her faith and her sanity. She'd prayed often, wondering when she'd see her brother again in some afterlife, or whether she'd die alone and unburied. If there were a higher power, why would He condemn her to loneliness?

Why would He condemn her to inevitable death? She still hadn't decided why that could be.

Reginald had been the first to find her. He'd located her in a flower shop, where she'd been hiding behind the counter with a knife and a bag full of supplies. He'd coaxed her out, brought her to the lumberyard, and promised her safety, introducing her to the others. In hindsight, he probably only wanted someone to help guard the gates.

She should never have followed him.

But how was she to know how violent he'd turn out to be?

They walked toward the massive, brick building. The school was several floors high, set back from the road, surrounded by a parking lot that spilled into a larger paved area around back. Sandy looked for cars, but didn't see any.

Only maintenance workers were likely to have been in the building. That might make it a safe stronghold. They could rest and gather supplies before moving on. Hopefully, they'd find a more stable vehicle than the truck.

They detoured from the road into the parking lot, keeping quiet. Simon kept the flashlight off. Sandy searched the dark windows on all floors of the building, expecting to hear hissing, hungry creatures waiting for a meal, but heard no clues that the building was occupied. The parking lot and the front entrance were silent and still.

"Let's check the back," Simon whispered.

Cautiously optimistic, Sandy followed him as he led the group from the front of the building to the rear. The lot was empty save a single vehicle occupying a spot near the rear entrance.

Simon appraised it from a hundred feet away. He halted.

"What is it?" Sandy hissed.

"Someone's inside." Simon raised his pistol, pointing at the vehicle and creeping closer.

Sandy motioned for the others to stay back. She hung behind Simon, holding her breath. She readied her knife. From the faint light of the moon, she made out a beat-up sedan. She couldn't see any more details than that.

Simon flicked the flashlight on, shining its beam over the car, revealing a sprinkle of glass by the driver's side window and a flat tire. He moved the light up to the driver's side door, illuminating a half-eaten face.

Sandy jumped. It looked like the person had been there for days. The person's face was gray and missing pieces, probably scavenged by birds and predators.

"Poor bastard," Sandy whispered.

Having determined nothing threatening was inside the vehicle, Simon walked up and inspected the car. "It's got a flat, but there might be a spare. The keys are in it. Let's see if it starts."

Sandy watched as Simon reached through the window and past the corpse. The flashlight moved, exposing a tangle of black hair, a thin flannel shirt. The person had probably been a maintenance worker. Sandy had seen plenty of corpses, but something about this one, alone in a parking lot, was especially unsettling.

Simon found a key in the ignition and turned it. The vehicle clicked but didn't turn over.

"Dammit," he said. "Looks like we're going inside."

The keys from the dead maintenance worker's car opened the school. Simon swung the back door open slowly, aiming his gun into a silent, dark hallway.

"I'll go first," he said, leading with the pistol.

The others followed. Sandy smelled the distinct odor of bleach from a set of bathroom doors, as if the school had been cleaned prior to the infection. Most of the classroom doors were open. They swept each one with the flashlight. When they were finished checking, Hector took a staggering step, catching himself on the wall.

"Hector!" Marcia whispered.

"I'm sorry. I'm just a little woozy," he replied.

Simon motioned to one of the doors labeled 'Break Room'. "Why don't you go in there and wait while I check the rest of the building?" he said.

"Are you sure?" Sandy asked.

"Yes. I'll be fine. I'll come back as soon as I'm done," Simon said.

He handed Sandy the bag of food he'd been carrying. Sandy took it as he headed off down the hallway without a word. She watched his flashlight disappear.

"Come on," Marcia said, watching him go. "He wouldn't have given us the food if he planned on leaving. Let's get Hector to a place where he can lie down."

Sandy followed the others into the break room. The moon shone through the windows, illuminating coffee machines, a microwave oven, and condiments on the counters. In the center of the room were a couch and several chairs. A foul smell grew worse as they got farther into the room. Marcia coughed. Sandy saw what looked like a plate of food that had been left out on the counter.

"Someone missed dinner," Hector said, attempting a smile.

"I don't think the smell is just from that," Sandy said, pointing at an oversized refrigerator. "Everything inside is probably rotten. We shouldn't open the door."

"Come on over to the couch," Marcia said, directing Hector toward it. "You should rest, honey."

"I'm fine," Hector said.

Despite protesting, he sat down with a sigh of relief. Marcia and Anabel sat next to him, keeping him company. After shutting and locking the door, Sandy found some napkins on the counter and gave them to Marcia. She took them gratefully, dabbing the remainder of the blood from Hector's face.

Sandy looked out across the parking lot, afraid that they might've drawn more creatures with the noise they'd made earlier, but all she saw were the silhouettes of the mountains and the empty, lifeless road.

Her mind wandered to the dead, half-eaten man in the car. If they hadn't left the lumberyard, she had no doubt that they would've died, too—either from the creatures, or from Reginald.

"Thank God we got away," Marcia said, echoing Sandy's thoughts.

"And we have food and water, too," Sandy added, setting her and Simon's bags on the counter. "Things could be worse."

"I feel awful for Finn," Hector said. "He shouldn't have died like that."

"We did what we could," Marcia said with a quiet sniffle.

Marcia hugged Anabel tight. Anabel remained quiet, burying herself in her mother's embrace. It seemed like she was in shock. Why wouldn't she be? The events since the infection had rattled all of them, forcing them to endure things no one should have to face. Sandy listened as Simon's footsteps in the hallway get quieter. A door creaked, and the hallway fell silent.

"Do you think we'll be able to find a vehicle in the morning?" Hector asked.

"I hope so," said Sandy. "Going into the mountains on foot would be even more dangerous than staying here."

"I wish we had some more weapons," Hector said.

Sandy walked over to the counters and sifted through the plastic utensils. She opened a few drawers and quietly rifled through them, but she couldn't see much in the dark. She'd have to wait for Simon.

"If we can survive the night, maybe we can check the utility shed," Sandy said. "I saw one in back."

She doubted the school would have much weaponry. But they'd search just the same. She walked back to the others and leaned against one of the walls.

"You did a brave thing," Hector said out of the blue.

"What do you mean?"

"Rescuing Dan and Quinn." Hector nodded. "I'm not sure I would've had the guts to do that. You probably saved their lives."

"I hope so. It was the best I could do for them, given the situation. I hope Reginald didn't find them."

Sandy closed her eyes. The headache she'd had earlier had subsided, but her arms were sore. She'd heard that the aftereffects of a collision could sometimes take days to appear. She hoped she was experiencing the worst of it. Staring into the dark, her thoughts roamed to Ben. She wondered how things would've turned out differently if her brother had been here. Where would they be? Would they already be someplace far away?

She still saw his snarling, twisted face coming at her.

A gunshot ripped the thought away.

"What was that?" Hector asked, sitting up from the couch.

"Simon," Sandy said frantically.

13

ANDY RAN TO THE BREAK room door, as if an onslaught of creatures might burst through it. She put her body weight against it. But the hallway was silent. She no longer heard footsteps, or any sign that Simon was alive.

"Where the hell is he?" Hector whispered, taking up a position next to her.

"I don't know."

One part of her wanted to rush into the hallway and determine if Simon was okay. The other knew she should remain in silence, preserving their safety.

She looked across the room, catching sight of Marcia's and Anabel's trembling silhouettes. Looking out the windows and into the parking lot, Sandy saw nothing that might've caused the noise.

One of the creatures might be inside. Or maybe something else happened?

Simon would've yelled for help, wouldn't he? Sandy swallowed and tried to reassure herself that nothing was wrong, even though her heart galloped with fear. She put her ear against the door.

A thump from the end of the hallway gave her a spike of fear.

Sandy looked around the room, locating the couch and chairs. Reinforcing the thin entrance might be the only thing that saved them from being eaten. But Sandy was frozen in place. The instinct to stay still was greater than the motivation to move.

Another noise sounded in the hallway. It sounded like a door clicking shut. Something scratched the floor at the end of the hallway. Sandy strained her ears, resisting the urge to call Simon's name, fearful she'd lure something else instead.

Hector's face was little more than a featureless oval.

A knock rattled the door.

Sandy stifled a cry as a thin beam of light appeared in the crack underneath the frame.

"It's me," Simon hissed.

"One of those things was on the second floor, but I took care of it. I found this in the nurse's office," Simon said, handing over a medical kit as they let him in. "I figured we could use more supplies."

Sandy watched Simon. He didn't appear to be injured. She took the kit and stashed it near one of the bags of food.

"The gunshot had us worried," she admitted. "What the hell happened?"

"There was a broken window in one of the classrooms on the first floor," Simon said. "It looks like one of those things had slithered through it. I moved a few desks in front of the opening to help stop others from getting in. Then I locked the door. Hopefully the building helped muffle the gunshot."

Sandy blew a nervous breath. Her uneasy nerves had become the norm, and they'd saved her life more than once. Looking at the door, she asked, "What do you think, Simon? Will we be safe for the night?"

Simon paused. "I think so. If we see anything coming, we have a few exits to choose from. I made sure all the entrances are locked." He held up the set of keys he was carrying.

Feeling more relaxed, Sandy exhaled. Exhaustion had been riding on her shoulders all day. It'd be good to sleep, even though she wasn't sure she'd be able to. With the immediate danger over, she felt a pang of hunger. Meals had become a task, to be taken care of in between running and surviving.

"Is anyone hungry?" she asked.

"I could use a drink," Hector admitted.

Sandy opened one of the bags of safe food and began digging. Simon assisted with his flashlight. Inside she found bottles of water and provisions wrapped in red packaging—supplies that had once belonged to the agents, the people who had perpetrated the contamination, according to Dan.

"We should ration it," she said, as if someone might argue. No one did. She passed out enough water bottles so that each person had his or her own.

Having accepted a bottle of water, Simon turned off his flashlight and hunched down on the floor next to Sandy. A different type of silence settled over the room, now that Simon had joined them.

"I probably should've said this earlier, but I'm sorry for what happened at the lumberyard." He cleared this throat.

The people in the room stayed quiet. No one accepted the apology. They just listened.

"I want to say there are reasons for it, but they're probably just excuses." Simon paused to take a deep breath. "Watching my sister die in Tucson was one of the hardest things I've ever faced. And the things I saw afterward were just as bad. I know we've all seen similar things, and I'm not saying I'm special. But I think something inside of me broke at that moment, and that led me to make some selfish decisions at the lumberyard."

Hector cleared his throat and clung to his family. After a pause, he said, "I appreciate you owning up to that, Simon."

Simon continued. "Hearing all those things Dan said about the agents made me nervous. To think that someone caused this intentionally was almost impossible to believe. Or maybe I didn't want to believe it. I don't expect you to trust me right away. But I hope we can work together. Nobody else should have to die like Finn did."

"Of course not," Marcia said, making the sign of the cross. "Let's hope we can keep safe."

Some of the tension seemed to deflate from the room as Simon drank from his water bottle. He seemed as relieved as the others, now that he'd aired some of his thoughts. He cleared his throat. "Do you think we're really immune, like Dan said?"

"If so, it wouldn't matter what we ate or drank," Sandy said. "But we shouldn't take any chances."

"That's a smart idea. We don't know how long the infection takes to kick in," Hector agreed.

"The fact that we're still here is a miracle," Marcia agreed quietly from the couch. "Someone must be watching over us."

Sandy uncapped her water and took a small swig. She swallowed, trying to remember the last uninterrupted rest she'd had.

Anabel's small voice piped up beside Marcia. "Can we eat now, Mom? I'm hungry."

They chuckled nervously. Sandy reached back into the bag and pulled out a package, reading the label aloud. "Crackers," she said. "That sounds great about now. Doesn't it, Anabel?"

"Yes."

Sandy smiled. Despite what they'd been

through, they'd escaped the lumberyard. They'd survived the truck issues and gotten to the school building. Aside from some cuts and bruises, they were relatively intact. She allowed a smile to linger on her face as she passed out the food to the people in the room. They ate in silence, each person running through the events that had led them there. When they were finished, Hector stood and offered his family the couch.

"Why don't you rest here," he told Marcia and Anabel. "I'll take the first watch, since I need to stay awake anyway."

"Someone should watch you," Marcia scolded. "What if you fall asleep by accident? You still might have a concussion."

Simon cut in. "I'll keep an eye on you."

"You will?" Hector asked.

"I'm already wide awake," Simon continued. "And besides, I don't think I'd be able to sleep, after killing that thing upstairs."

"I know the feeling," Sandy said. "The adrenaline of killing those things in the street still has me wide awake. I can take second shift, if you'd like."

"We shouldn't need much more than that," Simon said. "It'll be daylight soon. We can search the school again in the morning and figure out a plan. There have to be more cars close by."

"I saw a utility shed in back," Sandy repeated.

"That sounds good. We should check it."

"I'm just glad we're out of the lumberyard," Sandy said.

"I hope we never see Reginald again," Marcia agreed.

The group settled into the most comfortable places they could find. Sandy lay on an area rug on the floor, using a bag of packaged food to prop up her head. Marcia and Anabel lay on the couch cushions, while Hector lay on the couch without pillows. Simon took a spot in a chair by the window, looking out over the vacant, moonlit parking lot, the gun in his lap.

"I'll check on you from time to time," Simon told Hector.

"Sounds good," Hector replied. "Goodnight, everybody."

14

REGINALD STARED AROUND HIM AT the darkened city. Never in his life had he wanted to see lights so badly—some sign that his pursuits weren't pointless. He'd have to turn around soon. They'd been driving for almost an hour, and they'd been away from the lumberyard for way too long. He didn't trust Simon. And he certainly didn't trust Hector, Sandy, or the others. He wiped a band of sweat from his forehead.

They were probably already plotting against him, stealing his things.

More than likely, Dan was over the mountains, heading to some other town.

Reginald had wasted too much time pursuing that other vehicle.

He'd killed his chance at revenge.

Dammit.

Billy and Tom shifted in their seats, nervously watching the road. Their confidence seemed to have eroded after the confrontation with those people in the restaurant. Billy and Tom were weak. Useless. Reginald had a good mind to drop them off somewhere and let them find their way back. He doubted they'd survive until morning.

"We should turn around," Billy tried,

measuring his words. "I don't think we're going to find them."

"I'm checking Route 191 first," Reginald said after a pause. "We'll see if we can see lights in the city when we get some elevation on the mountains."

Billy and Tom exchanged a look that they thought Reginald didn't see. His anger flared as he thought about how useless their trip had been.

Thick, sloping rock faces appeared to the right of the vehicle as he ascended the mountain road, creeping toward the road's shoulder. There were no guardrails. He looked over the edge, wondering if Dan's car had ended up in some ditch.

Maybe I scared the fucker so bad he ran off the road.

That thought almost made Reginald laugh.

Maybe I'll find him in time to finish him off.

"Watch out!" Billy shouted.

Too late, Reginald swerved as one of the creatures appeared in the road. The Buick jerked to the side. Reginald started to yell, but he didn't have time to formulate a sentence before they were in the air. He clipped the creature, sending it tumbling off the mountain.

And then they were following it.

He pumped the brakes and turned the wheel. Nothing happened. The headlights pierced the empty air in front of him as the car turned sideways, throwing Reginald into Billy. He regurgitated the crackers he'd eaten earlier, projectile-vomiting sideways onto his friend.

Billy's and Tom's screams filled the air as the car kissed the mountain ravine and slid. Reginald tried to scream, but before he could, his world went black.

PART TWO
INHERIT THE WASTELAND

15

ANDY DIDN'T REALIZE SHE'D FALLEN asleep until she'd woken up in the middle of a large room.

People strode by her in all directions. Some were clients from her salon; others were neighbors from her apartment building. Some were people she'd never met. Their features were blurry as they hurried into a room she couldn't see. She tried to turn, but her legs were rooted in place.

Someone screamed.

Sandy clenched her teeth and forced herself to turn.

The walls felt like they were moving. Behind her, a large archway led into a white-walled room. Several creatures were quietly feeding on the people she'd seen walking by. None were screaming. None were defending themselves. They succumbed to their fates as if they were enjoying a spa, rather than being ripped apart and consumed. Blood soaked the floor, puddling around the dying people.

Someone bumped her arm. Sandy startled and looked left.

One of her neighbors — Marc, a short man with a shaved head — walked past her without a word.

She opened her mouth, trying to warn him not to walk in the other room, but she had no voice. Her legs were frozen as she tried to run after him. She watched in horror as he kept walking, stepping through the archway, only to be pulled to the floor and consumed. He fell so that he was facing Sandy, staring at her with hollow eyes as the creatures dug into his stomach, pulled out his insides, and feasted. His eyes went from alive to dull. Sandy felt a well of emotion as she cursed whatever force prevented her from moving.

Another bump startled her. She looked to the right to find her brother.

Ben. *Ben!*

Ben lit up at seeing her. His brown hair hung over his eyes, and his smile was as genuine as she remembered. Sandy's heart pounded with joy at seeing him again. She made a move to reach out to him, to hold him. Instead of returning the gesture, Ben lowered his eyes as if to apologize, and then walked past her, heading toward the killing room.

No!

Sandy's joy turned to terror as she watched Ben pass through the archway filled with blood and gore and pieces of people she knew. She fought against the force that was holding her down, willing her legs to move, but her efforts were useless. She couldn't move. She couldn't talk. Frantic tears rolled down her cheeks as she watched the creatures pull Ben to the ground. His legs buckled; his arms swayed, but he did nothing

T.W. Piperbrook

to stop the tearing hands or the vicious teeth. He succumbed to his fate without resistance, consumed without a fight.

Finally, Sandy managed a scream.

The sound was shrill, long, and piercing — nothing like her own. She screamed for what felt like forever, until hands tugged at her shoulders, consoling her. But they weren't consoling her. They were waking her up.

Sandy's eyes snapped open as a frantic voice whispered in her ear.

"Sandy! Get up! Something's wrong!"

16

MOANS FILLED THE AIR AS Sandy came alert. She was still in the dark break room at the elementary school. Marcia was waking her up, motioning to the windows. Sandy looked over to find creatures' hands sliding up and down the pane, searching for a way in. Every so often, one of the hands would slap the window, causing her a jolt of panic.

Looking around, Sandy found the huddled shapes of the rest of her companions hiding behind the couch. She sat up quietly, located her knife, and crawled to join them. Marcia was right behind her.

When they reached the couch, Sandy heard a thin whimper from the smallest shadow. Hector was holding Anabel close, his hand clamped over her mouth to try and quiet her. Her anxious breathing filled the air.

The creatures continued smacking the windows. Sandy heard the screeches of others walking the property, searching for survivors. Her heart pounded as she tried to determine how long she'd slept. It couldn't have been long. The room was still black, save the light of the moon that illuminated the silhouettes of the things around her. Across the room, she saw the remnants of the meal they'd eaten before bedding down. Past them were the counters and cabinets. It felt like she'd awoken into a continuation of her nightmare.

She wasn't sure which was worse.

The creatures increased their violent banging, as if they knew what was on the other side of the glass. Had they seen Hector or Simon? Sandy didn't know. It certainly felt as if the creatures knew exactly where they were. She looked across the room at the door, trying to recreate the layout of the school in her mind, planning an escape route.

A loud slap on the window made her jump. The others stiffened. Sandy peered up slowly, watching one of the creatures tap the glass. The fear in the room was a tangible, living being, hovering over them, waiting to strike. Sandy gripped her knife, waiting for the sound of shattering glass that would signal her to move, to fight, to run.

All at once, hands slid off the glass and the noises subsided. The groans moved farther away. Sandy heard footsteps as the creatures changed direction.

"They're passing through," Simon whispered, just loud enough that they could hear him. "I don't think they saw us."

Sandy swallowed as the creatures moved farther down the building, testing more windows. She recalled the broken pane in the classroom that Simon had barricaded the night before, having the sudden fear that one of the creatures would find it, knock it open, and lead the others inside.

They waited in the same position for what felt like forever, until Sandy's legs were cramped and her hands lost circulation from holding the knife so tightly. And then the noises were far enough away that she could barely hear them, blending with the sounds of night insects and the subtle gusts of the wind.

Simon sat up and blew a relieved breath.

"Hector and I saw them coming a few minutes ago," he explained, a little more loudly now that the creatures were gone. "We woke everyone up in case we needed to fight or run."

Sandy nodded. She got up slowly, peering over the couch. The grass and the parking lot were vacant. She scurried over to the windows, keeping a few feet away from the glass, as if they might explode inwards and admit the creatures. Her fear was that one of them was hovering quietly outside, waiting to signal the others. But she knew they weren't that intelligent or coordinated. At least, not that she'd encountered so far. The night was quiet and still. Deep in the distance, she saw a few shapes stalking down the road.

"They're leaving," she affirmed. "Do you want me to take a shift?"

"You only slept an hour," Hector said. "Why don't you get some more rest?"

Sandy started to argue, but Hector insisted. Marcia and Anabel settled back into the couch, relieved, but shaken. Sandy reclaimed her spot on the floor, wondering how she'd fall back to sleep with the adrenaline still coursing through her. She closed her eyes. After a long while of thinking and listening, she drifted.

This time, she didn't dream.

17

WHEN SANDY OPENED HER EYES, Simon was stationed at the window, shielding his eyes from the morning sun. Hector was searching the drawers and cabinets in the break room. Sandy felt a wave of guilt as she realized that neither had woken her up to take a shift.

"You let me sleep," she told them.

"We figured you could use the rest." Hector smiled and turned from sifting through one of the drawers. He held up a kitchen knife, tucking it into his waistband along with his other knife.

Sandy blinked and sat up. Most of her nights lately were spent battling nightmares, or expecting to be stirred. She was surprised to find that she was more rested than usual. She glanced over to find Anabel quietly eating some crackers with her mother. Marcia sat behind her, untangling knots from her daughter's hair.

"How'd you sleep?" Sandy asked them.

"Not great, but a little," Marcia said, as she put the package of crackers back in one of the bags.

Sandy turned to Hector, who was sliding one of the drawers shut. "Did you find anything else?"

Hector shook his head. "No. An elementary school isn't exactly a storehouse for weapons." He smiled grimly. "We checked the rest of the rooms while you were sleeping. We were able to see a little better in the daylight."

Sandy stood and walked over to where Simon was standing at the windows. He pointed at several smudged, dirty handprints on the panes.

"We got lucky last night," he said.

"Thank God they didn't see us," Sandy agreed.

She looked out the window, imagining a plague of creatures storming up the road, intent on breaking into the school, but the road was empty. The mountains stood like distant sentinels, providing a comforting landmark. For a moment, she was almost able to pretend that they were a group of travelers on a trip, heading out to go camping. But she knew better.

"I was thinking we could check the utility shed, like you suggested," Simon said. "Maybe we'll get lucky and find some oil for the truck, and something to patch it."

"Maybe it'll have some tools," Sandy added.

"What if we don't find anything?" Marcia asked from behind them. "Will we still be able to drive the truck?"

"It'll probably overheat quickly. We can take our chances, if we have to. Hopefully we can find another vehicle in the mountains before that happens. I don't think traveling on foot is the smartest move. Especially after what we saw last night."

Sandy nodded. She looked at the others, then

T.W. Piperbrook

at the walls around them. After the visit from the creatures the night before, the school felt safer than going outside. For a moment, she considered the possibility of staying. But she knew that would only be a temporary solution. Looking at the worried faces of the others, she wondered if they were mulling over the same things.

"Does everyone agree we should leave?" she asked, posing the question to the group.

Hector looked at his family and nodded. "We understood the risks when we left. We need to find help. The supplies we have will only last so long."

"I agree," Marcia added.

"Are you feeling any better today, Hector?" Sandy asked.

"Much," Hector said, touching his forehead. Sandy noticed most of the blood had been cleaned off. At the same time, his eyes had the puffy appearance of someone who hadn't slept.

"You still look tired, though," Sandy observed.

"Why don't Sandy and I check the utility shed, while you and your family rest a bit more?" Simon suggested. "We'll make sure no creatures are in the area. Then we'll come back and get you."

Hector opened and closed his mouth as if he were about to argue. Finally, he said, "Okay, but if you run into any trouble, please let us know. We'll keep watch out the front window. If we see anything, we'll alert you."

"Sounds good," Simon said.

18

S ANDY AND SIMON WALKED DOWN the empty hall of the school and toward the back of the building. The sound of their footsteps reinforced the feeling that they were the only survivors left in the world. Sandy looked around at the walls. They were filled with drawings and projects made by the students. She admired paper plates turned into human faces, Styrofoam cups turned into insects, and superhero finger paintings with various colors. She prayed the children who made them were somehow alive and safe.

That sentiment led to anger. The agents — the men in white coats — were callous and uncaring. She'd seen enough of their destruction to know that. In the time she'd been in St. Matthews, she'd watched children and adults infected, their bodies and minds warped by the contamination.

The same thing could've happened to Anabel. It could happen to any of them.

Sandy prayed that they were immune, as Dan had theorized. She followed Simon out the back door as they walked into the parking lot. The sun was warm and misleading, promising normalcy, as if today might be any other day, and she might be enjoying a coveted day off instead of fighting for survival. Sandy couldn't envision things ever returning to normal. Not now, and certainly not soon.

They moved in the direction of the utility shed, which was located at the rear south corner of the schoolyard, a few hundred yards from the main building. Sandy swallowed the pit in her stomach as they passed the half-eaten man in the car. He'd fallen forward and hung over the steering wheel, as if he'd finally given up. Or maybe more scavengers had found him. Sandy shuddered.

Simon's shoulders heaved as he kept a brisk pace. His t-shirt was stained with blood and sweat. He kept silent, holding his gun, intent on his mission rather than making comfortable conversation. Sandy found herself more at ease with him after his confessions the previous night. Although she still had a degree of wariness, she trusted him as much as she trusted anyone else in this new world.

Simon was helping them, and for now, that was enough.

They kept to the parking lot's edge, looking over their shoulders, keeping an eye on the desert. Unlike at night, they had a clear view of their surroundings.

When they reached the utility shed, Simon located the key on the maintenance worker's keychain. He unlocked the door, taking a stance as he pushed it open with his foot. Junked-out lawn mowers, weed whackers, and garden tools greeted them. He and Sandy stepped in.

"It doesn't look like anyone's been in here in a while," Simon observed as he looked at the neat, organized shelves on the walls. He pointed at two shovels hung on hooks. "We might be able to use those if we take them."

"For sure," Sandy agreed as she looked around further, noticing a garden rake on the wall and a box cutter on a small table. None of the weapons were ideal, but they were better than fighting with bare hands, and a welcome addition to the knives they carried. They'd take them.

"The true question now is whether we can find some tools and oil," Simon said, pursing his lips and looking around.

They perused the shelves and racks for something that might get the truck going, but didn't find much. Bags of fertilizer, topsoil, and mulch were stacked in a corner. Simon knelt next to a cardboard box and rifled through it. Sandy watched him take out a dusty baseball glove. He stopped to examine it. An expression of sadness crossed his face as he turned it over in his hands.

"Were you a baseball player?" Sandy asked.

Simon slowly exhaled. "No. My sister played. Softball."

Simon blinked hard and set the glove on the ground.

"I'm sorry," Sandy said. "I know you were close."

"We were," Simon agreed. "I used to go to all her games. Growing up, our parents worked a lot, and we always supported each other. In many ways, it felt like we raised each other."

"Are your parents still alive?" Sandy asked, realizing Simon had never elaborated on the rest of his family.

"I haven't spoken to them in years," Simon said. "They live in Denver. But my sister was always there to support me."

For the second time since they'd left, she saw a crack in Simon's exterior. He wiped his face, but didn't say anything further.

Speaking of Simon's family hit Sandy with a memory of her own. She blew a breath. "Ben used to play baseball. We've talked about him several times, but I never told you that I killed him."

Simon looked up at her. His normally hard expression remained soft. "You don't have to tell me anything," he said.

"I'm not sure why, but I want to."

Whether it was the nightmare of Ben flooding back to her, or the kinship of the moment, she wasn't sure, but she started talking. Simon watched her while she spoke. He didn't comment or interrupt. He didn't judge. Sandy relayed the details about her parents' car accident when she was twelve, then she spoke about Ben, and how he was the only one to push her along when all she wanted was to give up.

"We didn't have any close relatives. For a

while, we lived with a distant aunt, but after a while, her sympathy ran out and we became a burden. As soon as we were old enough to live on our own, we moved out and got an apartment. Eventually we moved to St. Matthews. All Ben and I had was each other. When people in town started becoming infected, my first thought was to get back to him. I went back to our apartment complex, and that's when I found him in the hallway, eating someone."

"He turned," Simon surmised.

"Yes." Sandy swallowed the lump in her throat. "He was on top of Mrs. Lindblad, one of our neighbors. He'd already killed her. He was... chewing on her neck."

"What'd you do?"

Sandy told how she'd been forced to kill him. Then she relayed how she'd been forced to flee. "I never got a chance to bury him. I wanted to, but those things were everywhere. I had to get out. Just like we had to do with Finn."

Sandy didn't realize she was crying until the tears were streaming down her face and she could no longer speak. She turned to face the wall, unsure why she'd trusted this man over the others, especially after Simon's questionable actions. But she'd already told her story. There was no taking it back. She blinked, surprised when Simon got to his feet and gave her a hug.

The gesture was brief, but consoling.

"I'm sorry about your brother," he said, letting go.

"I had a dream about him last night. Maybe that's why I can't get him out of my head."

"The dreams are the worst part," Simon agreed. "When we wake up, we have to accept reality all over again."

They hung in silence for a moment, watching each other. Finally, Simon packed the baseball glove silently into the box, his eyes roaming to the wall. Sandy bit back memories of her own. Breaking free of her bad memories, she knelt down and searched through a box next to him. They found no oil, but they did locate a few tools for the truck.

They were just gathering things together when a car engine sounded in the distance.

Sandy looked around. For a moment, she was convinced she was hearing things, or that her memories were causing her to create noises. But Simon was swiveling, too.

"Is someone coming?" he asked, sneaking back to the door. He peered out, his expression changing from reflection to fear. Panic surged through Sandy as he hissed, "A minivan. It's coming toward the school."

19

EGINALD SQUINTED THROUGH AN ARRANGEMENT of colors as warmth hit his face. The last few syllables of some forgotten warning were on his tongue. He closed his mouth and tried clearing his throat, but couldn't muster any saliva.

Where am I?

Reginald blinked as he came to consciousness. His vision cleared, revealing a spider web of crooked lines along the Buick's windshield. He tried to sit up, but his seatbelt held him in place. He didn't even remember putting the seatbelt on. The feeling of being trapped overtook him, but his sore muscles forced him to slow down and think.

His lap felt warm. Years of experience with similar feelings — side effects of drugs — made him wonder if he'd let his bladder loose. He looked down, but instead of dark urine, he saw Billy lying on top of him. Blood gushed from Billy's head onto Reginald's pants. Billy's face was mashed and unrecognizable. Reginald dry-heaved and tried to get away from the dead man. Before he could, Billy latched onto him.

"Get off of me!" Reginald yelled, flailing wildly.

It took him a second to realize it wasn't Billy

grabbing him, but that it was his seatbelt. Reginald reached around Billy's body, frantically hitting the clasp and undoing it. When he freed himself, he noticed someone else in his peripheral vision. Reginald turned around, locating Tom. The man's head was bent over between his legs. He wasn't moving, either.

"Tom?" Reginald's voice was raspy, unsure. The man didn't answer him.

I'm the only one who survived.

A momentary sense of elation hit Reginald, tempered by the realization that he might be injured and not know it. He checked himself for wounds, but found only a few scrapes. Looking in the twisted rearview mirror, he saw some shallow cuts on his face. The blood on his pants seemed to be Billy's.

Reginald had no idea where he was. The last thing he recalled was driving up the mountains on Route 191, trying to spot Dan before heading back to the lumberyard. Even that memory was blurry and distorted, as if he couldn't trust it. Reginald reached for the door, peering out through the cracked windshield, noticing the thick, looming tree the car had wrapped around. Brush and foliage extended as far as Reginald could see. He'd reached the bottom of an incline.

I'm somewhere in the mountains.

Shifting out from underneath Billy, Reginald wriggled out of the vehicle and found purchase in the dirt and grass. His legs were shaky. He held the top of the door to keep upright, peering back in at his companions, but they remained in the same positions. A glint of metal on the floor reminded him of the gun he'd been carrying. Reginald reached in and grabbed it. Another gun was on the floor underneath Billy, wedged beneath the dead man's leg. He didn't see Tom's weapon. Leaving the door open, Reginald made his way around the car, gritting his teeth at a few sparks of pain in his legs. He was sore, but nothing felt broken. It seemed like the few scratches and cuts were his only injuries.

He reached the passenger's side door and tugged on the handle, grunting as he reached inside and claimed Billy's gun. As he got out, he gave a cursory glance at the totaled car, wrapped so tightly around the tree that he couldn't imagine what it had looked like when it drove. He'd never get it working.

He had no transportation. No food. All Reginald could think about was the lumberyard.

He needed more meth.

20

SIMON HELD THE PISTOL IN his hands as he peered through the crack in the door of the utility shed, fear melting the sympathy in his expression. Sandy joined him, looking out as the sound of the car engine got closer. From their vantage point, Sandy saw only the sliver of road past the school that a few inches of the open door allowed, and the distant form of the approaching vehicle. She knew better than to open the door all the way.

"What should we do?" she hissed.

"Stay put. Maybe it'll keep going," Simon said, but his tone indicated that he wasn't sure.

They hung next to the door as the car approached, waiting for a glimpse of whomever was inside. Sandy realized that, while her initial reaction was fear, there was a possibility the vehicle contained someone who was willing to help.

Maybe someone is looking for survivors.

She tabled that hope as she saw the vehicle's occupants. Two men with guns were inside, leaning out the windows and surveying the landscape, their faces hard and determined. The car slowed and its brake lights flashed as it approached the school. Her heart sunk.

"Shit," Simon muttered.

"They must've seen our truck down the road," Sandy guessed. "That means they might've found the rest of our supplies."

That fear was made worse by the fact that the men were coming closer. The van slowed and turned into the school parking lot. Within seconds, the vehicle was out of view. The brakes squeaked. A door opened. A man said something she couldn't hear, and footsteps pounded the pavement in front of the building.

"They'll find Hector and his family," Sandy hissed, her pulse pounding behind her temples.

"I'm sure they'll hide," Simon tried, but his shaky voice showed he wasn't convinced.

A moment later, glass shattered and the men burst into the school.

21

B Y THE TIME REGINALD HAD reached the top of the incline, he'd forgotten all about Billy and Tom. His companions were worthless. They'd proven that in the city. He'd be better off without them. He concentrated on pushing his legs up the hill, using roots and shrubs to catch his balance. Though he wasn't sure where he was going, Reginald knew he needed to reach the road. That would give him the best chance of figuring out where he was, and making it back to the lumberyard.

That would get him back to his stash.

The sun beat down overhead, baking blood and sweat into stains on his clothes. He'd never get rid of that foul odor. Reginald cursed. He tried to remember the last time he'd showered, but couldn't. Staying alive—and high—had become more of a priority.

He grunted as his ankle twisted on a rock. He pushed off it and caught his balance, sending the stone tumbling down the ravine as fresh pain sparked in his leg, making him angry.

Dan and Quinn did this to me.

Reginald gritted his teeth as he found someone to blame. Here he was, grunting and sweating like a pig while they stole away, laughing. They'd evaded him like he was nothing. And the people at the lumberyard were no better. Hector and the rest of them probably thought he was dead. They were probably locking him out and stealing his food and supplies.

And his meth.

Fuckers.

Anger propelled him harder and faster, until he was at the lip of the road, scrambling and pulling himself to the asphalt. He looked up and down the vacant roadway, but saw no one.

Of course he didn't.

Reginald was alone on this god-forsaken mountain. Hell, probably in this whole town. His high was long gone, and Reginald was agitated. Jittery. It'd be a long walk back to the lumberyard, unless he could secure a vehicle. He carried the rifle and pistol pointed in front of him as he stole down the street.

22

ECTOR HUGGED HIS FAMILY AS he listened to the armed men burst into the downstairs hallway of the elementary school. He'd been watching them from the window. He'd seen their guns. He knew the looks on the men's faces. They were the same looks he'd seen on some of the people in New Mexico, and then St. Matthews, after the infected had spread and the weak had been separated from the strong.

Hector liked to think he and his family were some of the strong, but having witnessed some of the brutal things people could do, he knew they had to be smart, too. Hector had learned there were times when they should hold their ground, and times when they should hide.

Now was one of those latter times.

Between his injury and their lack of weapons, he and his family wouldn't be able to get the upper hand.

A few moments earlier, Hector had led Marcia and Anabel to the second floor, in hopes of gaining another layer of protection. He looked around the room in which they'd shut themselves. Broken copying machines, old rotary telephones, and shelves filled the room. They were in a supply room with no windows. At the time, it had seemed safer than the classrooms with their windows and glass panes in the doors. Now he questioned that logic.

Hector stared at the door across the room, which was locked with a thin bolt. He doubted the door would withstand a well-placed kick. In Hector's hands was the largest of his knives and a telephone. It was a last-ditch defense, good only for hurling at someone, should they break in. Marcia had her knife out, too.

He listened intently as the men's voices grew louder downstairs. They were working their way through the building. Doors banged against walls. Every so often, a desk scraped against the floor as the men ransacked a room. Hector wasn't sure what they were looking for, but he knew better than to risk himself and his family by coming out.

His last, desperate hope was that the men would skip the second floor.

Maybe they'll lose interest and move on.

Where were Sandy and Simon?

Hector knew better than to rely on his companions. If they were smart, they were hiding, too. Hector met Marcia's eyes as she looked between him and the door. If he could speak, he'd conjure some inspiring words that would give her and Anabel the courage to face yet another nightmare. Instead he could only listen as the men got closer, unwilling to risk it.

His heart sank as footsteps hit the stairs. The men got closer.

"Be quiet," he mouthed. Marcia and Anabel nodded, tears in their eyes. The men's conversation drifted down the hallway as they reached the second floor landing. Each footstep was a reminder of how fragile the family's position was. All they could do was listen and wait.

"This place brings back shitty memories," one of the men said, chuckling quietly. "I hated school."

"If we find something here, it'll be worth the detour," a second voice said. "We'll have plenty of time to stare at each other on the mountain."

"What if we can't find the place?"

"We have the map. And the notes they gave us."

"They might've been lying."

"Well, we can't ask them now." The second man laughed. "And besides, we'll find out soon enough, won't we?"

A door smashed against a wall down the hallway. "This place fucking stinks like bleach."

"Believe me, if we find someone to have a little fun with first, it'll be worth it."

Hector's blood ran cold. He tried to make sense of what the men were talking about. Whatever their conversation meant, they sounded as violent as some others they'd run into. He swallowed and herded his family behind him. He raised the telephone and the knife.

Shoes squeaked on the linoleum as the men kicked in another door.

"I'm telling you, whoever was here already left, Dwight."

"We'll check the rest of the floor first. Then we'll get the hell out of here."

Hector's hope turned to despair as the footsteps grew louder. It sounded like the men were a room away. He flexed his hands, preparing for what might be the last confrontation of his life.

23

SIMON AND SANDY PEEKED THROUGH the crack in the doorframe of the utility shed, hoping to determine the men's location. Bangs echoed from inside the building as the men made their way through the school. The smell of garden tools and cut grass filled Sandy's nostrils. She felt claustrophobic, trapped. She wanted nothing more than to leave the utility shed and get to Hector, Marcia, and Anabel.

"We need to help them," she whispered frantically to Simon.

"If we go out, we risk getting killed," Simon hissed. "We have to hope they'll stay hidden."

"What if they don't?"

A particularly loud crash made them both tense up. Simon wiped his face and blew a breath, thinking. After a few seconds, he said, "All right. Stay close and follow me."

Without giving her a chance to answer, Simon pushed open the door and ran in a crouch, making his way across the parking lot. Sandy followed, her pulse knocking violently as she anticipated the gunshot that would take her to the ground.

None came.

She looked toward the distant, tree-filled

mountains, hit with the sudden, selfish feeling to run. But losing Ben had taught her a lesson about guilt that she wouldn't soon forget.

She'd help her friends, even if it meant putting herself in danger. That was the promise she'd made, after she'd freed Dan and Quinn and hadn't gone with them.

Simon motioned her toward the building. Sandy swallowed the acidic taste in her throat and followed him as they reached the back entrance of the school in a quick dash. Soon they were standing at either side of the door. Inside, Sandy heard the muffled voices of men. It sounded like they'd already passed by the break room.

"They're upstairs," Simon mouthed.

Sandy clung to the hope that Hector and his family hadn't been found. Simon scooted over, hissing quietly in her ear, "Let's check the break room first. Maybe Hector and his family are still there. We can signal them and leave."

Sandy nodded. Simon unlocked the door and glanced into the building. The men continued kicking open doors on the upper floor. Simon mouthed the words, "one, two, three," and then they were whipping down the hallway.

Sandy's heart pounded like a jackhammer as she flew by classroom after classroom. Most of the doors hung open. In the middle of the hallway, she saw the break room where they'd slept. The door hung ajar. Sandy suppressed the thought that Hector, Marcia, and Anabel were inside, riddled with blood and bullets. But she hadn't heard gunshots. She hadn't heard shouts.

They had to be alive.

At least, she told herself that.

Sandy and Simon reached the door and peered cautiously inside. The couches and chairs had been moved sideways, but no one was there, as if the room was home to ghosts. The bags of food were gone.

Hector and his family took them.

The realization was both relieving and frightening. It meant Hector and his family were safe, at the moment. But the men would find them if they looked hard enough. And when they did—

A scream pierced the air.

The noise was high-pitched, terrified, and unmistakably Marcia's. Sandy and Simon raced back into the hallway.

24

R EGINALD WALKED UNTIL THE SUN rose in the sky and warm rays of heat penetrated the boughs of the trees. He was parched. He tried to determine what time of day it was. It felt like mid-day. In the time he'd been walking, he hadn't seen a car. Neither had he seen any signs of life.

But that made sense, now that the world was over.

He needed to find a car, or some unfortunate survivor he could convince to give him a ride. At least, he told himself that as he fought through his headache.

He ground his teeth together, a habit he'd picked up without realizing it, and pressed his lips together. His throat was so dry that he couldn't think about anything other than getting some water.

Reginald cursed as he walked down the road. His best chance was back at the lumberyard. He didn't know if he could wait that long for uncontaminated fluid. His hands shook as he held the rifle and the pistol in his hands, making him increasingly agitated. He looked up and down the winding, wooded road, wishing a car would appear and give him another option.

He'd gone another half mile when he saw a log cabin through the trees, a few hundred feet from the road. He chewed his lips and wandered from the road into the forest. Where there was a cabin, there might be cars, or maybe a stream or a brook nearby, something that would be safe to drink so he could quench his intolerable thirst.

He hated the woods.

25

MARCIA SCREAMED AS A BOOT hit the door. Hector shielded his wife and daughter, fear slamming his stomach. Marcia's scream had given them away, but they would've been discovered anyway.

"Stay back!" Hector shouted through the door, throwing as much ferocity into his voice as he could muster. He held the phone over his head as if it was a bomb he might set off, instead of a useless electronic device.

"Who's in there?" one of the men shouted, as if Hector might answer honestly. It sounded like the men had stepped back to regroup.

"Get back or I'll shoot!" Hector screamed, grabbing for a desperate ploy.

The men were quiet, as if they were contemplating what he'd said. He heard a few whispers, then a stifled laugh.

"If you had a gun, we'd know it by now," the second man said. "The people who aren't dead already aren't afraid to shoot."

The guess was accurate, though Hector would never admit it. "I'm going to warn you one more time, and the next warning is a bullet," he yelled. "Get the hell out of here!"

"You're on foot," the first man guessed, as if Hector hadn't spoken. "We saw your truck down the road. It looks like you need help. We'll give you a ride."

The hallway went silent. As much as Hector would like to believe the lie, he'd already heard the men talking. They were ill intentioned, like too many others in this new world. They'd boasted about killing others. At least, it sounded like it.

"The police are right up the road," the second man added. "We'll bring you to them."

Lies, Hector thought. He knew the rest of the force in St. Matthews was dead. Dan had passed that information along to Sandy. For all Hector knew, so were the police in every other town.

"We don't need help," Hector said, trying to control the waver in his voice. "I told you to get away from the door. We can manage just fine."

The hallway remained quiet. Hector prayed the men might leave. Instead, the door handle rattled. Anabel cried out in fright. Panic and rage surged through Hector. If he had a weapon, he'd shoot through the door, just like he'd promised, and he'd keep firing until these men were dead.

Footsteps echoed in the hall. Suddenly, the door caved and a boot appeared in the center. The boot twisted and turned as the man attached to it tried to pull it free. Hector looked around, pointing to a small space between a copier and a table where Marcia and Anabel could hide.

"Get in there!" he hissed.

Hector pressed himself flat against the wall as the boot retracted. He lifted the phone over his head. As soon as the door opened, he'd hurl it. Then he'd charge with his knife. He knew he was no match for a gun; his best hope was taking the men by surprise. He didn't have any other options. He couldn't let his family be subjected to the whims of these men.

The door burst open, smashing against the wall. Hector hurled the phone, watching it clatter uselessly in the hallway as the men retreated. Hector saw they were wearing jeans, boots, and grimy white t-shirts. They smiled at him. Desperation washed over him as he saw them looking past him at Marcia and Anabel.

"Leave them alone!" he cried.

Hector needed to do something. If he didn't, his family would be victimized. He'd seen enough people in similar situations to know that. The closest man was fifteen feet away. Hector held up his knife. If he could reach him in time, maybe he could do something. The man took a step closer, smiling as he raised his rifle and pointed it at Hector's chest.

"Stay back, you son of a bitch!" Hector yelled.

A gunshot ripped through the air, knocking into the man.

The man toppled sideways and landed on top of his weapon. The other shrieked in pain as a bullet tore through his calf. He dropped to the ground, too, losing his gun and crawling toward Hector and safety.

Hector wouldn't let him get to him or his family.

Hector tackled the man to the ground as he came through the doorway. His knife skittered from his grasp, but he didn't let that stop him. He swung a fist at the man, striking him in the face. He hit him again, and again, thinking of his family and all the people who had fallen prey to men with similar intentions. He thought of what this man would do if he reached them.

The man cried out in pain and struck back, thrusting his knee out, catching Hector in the groin. Hector doubled over and fell back. He heard footsteps and shouts in the hallway, but he didn't have time to confirm whom they belonged to. The man was reaching for something on his ankle. *A gun.*

Hector was about to dive for cover when another gunshot sounded and the man fell back to the floor. Looking up, Hector found Simon hovering in the entrance of the supply room, his pistol raised. His teeth were clenched, as if he might shoot the man again, even though the man was already dead.

"Are you hurt?" Simon asked.

"You saved us," Hector said, unable to contain the emotion in his voice.

"Are you okay, though?" Sandy asked.

"We're fine," Hector said, looking at his family to make sure.

Marcia and Anabel wiggled out from behind the copying machine and embraced Hector. Hector's body stung from the blows he'd taken, but the pain was nothing compared to what he'd feel if Simon hadn't stepped in. Sandy watched them worriedly.

Hector studied the two dead men on the floor, as if they might spring to life and attack him again. Their eyes were rolled back in their heads; last, venomous words stuck on their lips.

"We saw them pulling in when we were in the utility shed," Sandy explained. "We came as soon as we could."

Without another word, Sandy collected the men's weapons from the ground. She looked them over and handed a rifle to Hector. Hector didn't know a lot about firearms. He'd only used them a few times while guarding the shack at the lumberyard.

"Take it," Sandy said.

"I'm not the greatest shot," he admitted.

"Me, neither," Sandy admitted, holding the pistol she'd taken from the man's ankle holster. "But I have a feeling by the end of this, we're going to need to be."

S ANDY PATTED THE POCKETS OF the dead men on the ground while Simon acquainted Hector with the rifle. She grimaced as she rolled one of the dead men over. She'd patted down a few dead people in St. Matthews, but she'd always done it with a sick feeling in her stomach.

The first man's pockets were empty except for a can of chewing tobacco, a handful of lint, and a wallet. She slipped out his license and read the name. *Dwight Pickman.* The name meant nothing to her. She rifled through a stack of credit cards and membership licenses, but nothing stuck out. The man was the same as any other violent person she'd seen since the infection had hit, taking advantage of people's weaknesses, rather than trying to help. A bitter, angry pit took root in her stomach. The unprovoked cruelty of these men reinforced her disappointment in humanity.

This is how we treat each other when the walls break down? Like animals?

The second man's name was Samuel Black, according to his wallet. He had a set of keys and a folded piece of paper. Sandy took them and stepped back, as if he might come to life, reach over, and snatch them. Being around the dead men gave her a prickle of unease that she wanted to be rid of.

Marcia had taken Anabel away from the gory scene, calming her down at the end of the hallway. "It's going to be okay, honey," Marcia said. "We're going to be all right."

Sandy wondered how many times Marcia had told her similar things. Too many, she was sure. Having finished their conversation about the rifle, Simon and Hector walked over and rejoined Sandy.

"What did you find?" Simon asked.

"Some spare ammunition, and some keys," Sandy said. "And this." She held up a piece of paper and unfolded it, determining it was the page of an atlas with handwritten notes were scribbled along the edges.

"What the hell is that?" Simon wondered.

"I heard them talking," Hector said, furrowing his brow as he put something together. "It sounded like they killed some people and took it. They mentioned a room on the mountain, and a map. It sounded like someone made notes for them."

"A room in the White Mountains?" Sandy asked, furrowing her brow.

"I think so. I assumed they were headed to a hideaway of some kind."

"Can I see that?" Simon asked, reaching for the atlas page.

"Sure." Sandy handed it over. She watched as he traced his hand over the pictures and lines, reading the words scrawled on the side of the map.

"I've heard rumors of preppers creating bunkers in the mountains, usually in the vicinity of White Mountain Lake," Simon said. "Between the mountains and the thick forest, you could get lost and no one would ever find you, if you picked the right spot. We originally talked about getting away, but this might be another option if we can't find help."

"Can you read what it says?"

"It's a little hard to make out, but we might be able to decipher it."

"How far away is this place?" Sandy asked.

Simon paused as he studied the paper. "I'm not too familiar with the area, being from Tucson, but I've read some maps before. It looks like this place is about ten miles from here. If they have supplies there, chances are they'll be safe to eat. Most of these guys stockpile things for years."

"We can get supplies and decide what to do from there," Sandy added.

"Maybe we can wait it out until things are safer."

"How will we know that?" Hector asked.

"I'm not sure," Simon admitted, shrugging his shoulders. "It's an option, that's all."

Simon and Sandy watched Hector as he contemplated their words. He scratched his chin and looked at his family. "From everything we've seen, that sounds like a better plan than waiting here. I say we do it."

A soft wind blew through Sandy's hair as she surveyed the beat-up minivan. Simon crept toward the vehicle. The others hung back, pointing the weapons they'd taken from the dead men, cautiously watching. Although Sandy had only seen two men inside, she knew better than to trust that assessment. There might be others.

Simon scurried alongside the van and looked through the tinted windows. After a moment, he proclaimed it was empty.

Sandy exhaled. Not only was she grateful to be out of danger, but also she was grateful to be away from the dead men. She prayed they'd be the last violent people they'd meet, though she knew better than to believe it.

"It looks like they found the rest of the supplies from our truck," Simon pointed out, holding up some familiar red packages of food and water. "They must've stopped before they came here."

"That will save us the trip back," Sandy said gratefully.

27

EGINALD WALKED THROUGH THE TREES, falling against a few of them. Maybe he was more fucked up from the accident than he realized. Despite the aches in his body, he couldn't stop his thoughts from wandering. He needed water. He needed —

Reginald tensed as movement skittered through the trees. Was someone stalking him? He squinted from the glare of the sun, trying to determine who was hunting him down. He raised his rifle. Hearing nothing, he took a tentative step, startling several birds into taking flight from a distant perch. He whipped his gun in their direction. He looked all around, certain he'd find someone staring at him, or one of the creatures, salivating, waiting to pounce.

Nothing.

Mustering his courage, Reginald forced another step. If he saw someone, he'd shoot them. He'd take the fucker out, whoever it was. No one would harm him. He paused before walking further, realizing the forest had settled into the same quiet as before. He wiped sweat from his brow with his arm as he dismissed whatever illusion he'd convinced himself he'd seen.

He'd gone another twenty feet when something appeared through the trees. He stopped in his tracks, pointing his pistol and his rifle. A figure stood a hundred yards away, unmoving. Reginald saw glimpses of dark clothing and a hat. He couldn't make out any of the person's features. He tried to remain still, even though his body was shaking.

If you come any closer, motherfucker...

The person hung in the shadows, watching. Reginald waited and aimed. Whoever it was, he'd blast them back to whatever hell they came from. Despite his bravado, Reginald found himself glancing over his shoulder, gauging the distance to the road.

The person bounded toward him. Their feet crunched over leaves and branches as they skirted trees and scraggly brush, gaining ground. Reginald fired twice, sending bullets pinging off the trees. The person was moving too fast and too erratically to hit. Reginald swore and backpedaled a few steps, his face drenched with sweat. Between the glare of the sun and his shaking hands, he couldn't get off another shot. It seemed like there were two people running at him, even though he knew there was only one.

Dammit!

Hisses filled the air. The person—thing—got closer. Reginald saw a bearded, dirt-stained face underneath the hat, and hands outstretched in anticipation of digging into his flesh. The

T.W. Piperbrook

creature's eyes were black. He wouldn't let it get to him.

He fired off several more shots, landing one in the creature's arm. The thing swayed but kept coming, getting close enough that he could see its red, stained teeth before he fired again.

This time he struck the creature in the head and the thing toppled to the ground in a heap. He watched the creature as if it might come back to life, even though he'd obviously killed it. He blinked the sweat from his eyes, his heart racing so fast he could feel it through his body.

"Piece of shit," Reginald muttered, gaining some of his courage back.

He swiveled around the forest as if more might be waiting to spring at him, even though the woods had gone silent. Satisfied he was alone, Reginald wiped his face and kept walking.

28

EFORE LEAVING THE SCHOOL, SANDY and the others repacked the food in the minivan, as well as the medical supplies Simon had found the night before. They also packed a few things from the utility shed: the shovels, the box cutter, and a few tools.

"You never know when we might need them," Simon said, as they shut the back door.

Sandy agreed. She looked over at her companions, grateful that they'd made it this far. Every day seemed like a gift in a world that didn't have many favors left to give.

"Do you want me to drive?" she asked, thankful for the rest she'd gotten.

"Sure," Simon said.

Sandy dug out the keys and got in the driver's seat. Hector, Marcia, and Anabel rode in back, while Simon took the passenger's seat, studying the atlas page.

Sandy clenched the wheel as they drove out of the elementary school parking lot and toward the distant mountains. The sun cast beaming rays onto the asphalt, creating a shimmering glare. She had to squint to see. Sandy took in their surroundings. The rising, majestic landscape seemed more suited for photographs than reality. The sloping mountains rose and fell gracefully, as if they were made of fluid rather than earth and stone, their sides speckled with trees and green foliage.

"I remember coming this way with my brother," Sandy recalled wistfully. "We used to take drives all the time when we first moved, before things got busy."

"They always do," Simon said.

"I'd give anything for one last drive with him."

"I'd been meaning to take a camping trip with my sister. I never thought I'd make it up here this way."

Sandy smiled grimly. "Have you ever been to the White Mountains?"

"No," Simon said. "I heard a lot about it, while living in Tucson. I know the camping is supposed to be really nice."

"How long have you lived in Tucson?"

"Only about a year. I was still getting used to the area."

Sandy nodded. She watched as several buildings passed by the roadside — one-story constructs that looked like they hadn't harbored life in years. Occasionally they drove past a splattered, gruesome carcass on the road as they got closer to the mountains. Sandy imagined fleeing survivors running over the things on their way to safety. She'd seen plenty of that in the beginning, back when there had been enough survivors that she couldn't count them all. Now they'd be lucky to find one.

She glanced down at the pistol in her lap, feeling safer with it in her possession. It was much better than the knife she was carrying. Simon held one of the dead men's rifles. He'd given his pistol to Marcia, while Hector took the other rifle.

They were armed better than they'd been before. At least that was a relief.

Thick, ponderosa pines sprung up as they curved onto Route 191, headed into the mountains. Sandy had envisioned taking this route many times, usually while keeping watch at the lumberyard, or huddled in some building in the center of town, praying she'd escape and find help. She'd dreamed of rescue so many times that it felt unreal to be driving here now.

St. Matthews was a wasteland, a place littered with bodies and bones and the remnants of a life that she knew was over. The sight of several creatures wandering in the woods reinforced that thought.

"Look out!" Anabel said from the backseat, pointing at one of them, who had sprung out into the road. Its black eyes surveyed the vehicle. Sandy swerved away from it. Another creature ran from the woods, tearing after the minivan.

"Jesus," Marcia mumbled.

"They seem more animal than human," Hector observed, leaning forward. "It's hard to believe these were somebody's neighbors, their friends."

"I miss the people back home," Marcia said with a sniffle.

"You're from Truth or Consequences, right?"

"Yes," Hector confirmed. "In New Mexico."

"Did you have a lot of family there?" Sandy asked them, sensing their sadness. Although they'd talked about their escape, she didn't remember hearing much about their relatives.

"We had some family." Hector lowered his head. "Marcia's aunt and uncle. And lots of friends in town. We tried finding them when this happened, but most of them were caught up in the rush of people trying to leave—the people who hadn't turned, of course. They didn't make it. We found Marcia's aunt and uncle in a line of cars a few blocks away from their house. Lots of others were killed alongside them."

"Hector didn't want to leave until he knew what happened to them," Marcia said.

"That was brave of you," Sandy said.

Hector sighed and hugged Marcia. "I thought I could save them. Maybe I should've known better. We spent several days sneaking from building to building, hiding from those things, but things only seemed to get worse. That's when we came to St. Matthews, hoping things would be better. I wish we were right."

Sandy nodded grimly.

They drove past a few other creatures lingering in the trees, who were watching intently, as if Sandy and her companions might pull over and open the doors, allowing them inside. Soon the creatures disappeared and they were left with only thick forest on either side of the road.

"Hopefully we'll see less of those things as we travel up into the mountains," Simon suggested.

Sandy clung to that thought as the road curved sharply upward. She wiped a line of sweat from her forehead. With the day getting hotter, the interior of the minivan was growing warmer, as well. Sandy rolled the window down as far as she dared. Looking in the rearview, she saw Hector, Marcia, and Anabel sweating, too.

Sandy flicked on the air conditioning, but the unit only growled, spitting hot air.

"I guess that doesn't work," Sandy said.

"Better than being stuck out there." Hector waved an arm, gesturing out the window.

They drove until the trees got thicker and shielded the vehicle from some of the heat. Signs warned of an altitude climb. A few marked turn-off roads that led to campgrounds and retreats. Sandy had been into the mountains before, but the lack of guardrails was still surprising. She'd heard of several accidents on the roadways, when camping and alcohol had mixed. Often people had gotten careless and forgotten their steep surroundings.

She looked over to find Simon studying the map.

"Any idea where I'm going?"

He furrowed his brow. "It looks like the map

directs us to a campground. Wherever this place is, most of the path will be on foot after that."

"That makes sense," Sandy said. "Whoever built it must've hidden it."

"Stay on the main road for now."

They drove for a while, taking the turns slowly to account for the dangerous travel. The campground signs seem to have gotten fewer and farther apart. The roads Sandy saw were little more than paths that wound to places they couldn't see.

A gasp from the backseat made her tense and hit the brakes. "What is it?" she asked.

She turned, noticing Hector pointing at something down the road. She followed his finger. A figure moved in the distance, but she couldn't make out many details. She swallowed and reduced speed. Simon sat forward, holding his rifle.

The vehicle slowed to a crawl.

With each rotation of the tires, Sandy made out a little more of the distant, moving figure. It was a woman, pinned to a tree at the edge of the road. Her long hair whipped back and forth over her face as she shrieked in agony. She waved desperate, pleading hands at them. It wasn't until they were twenty yards away that Sandy saw the long knife protruding from her belly.

"Oh my God!" Hector said.

"We have to help her!" Marcia cried.

Simon leaned forward and turned in his seat,

as if someone might be waiting to spring out and ambush them. Sandy saw no one in the vicinity.

"What do we do?" she hissed.

"Pull up slowly," Simon instructed. "Keep an eye out. We'll help her."

Sandy looked in the rearview mirror. The road was narrow enough that turning around wouldn't be easy. Looking back at the pinned person, she wondered what sort of monster would leave a person to bleed out and die. But she knew. People like the men they'd encountered at the elementary school, or some of the men they'd met in town.

She crept slowly as they approached the woman. The woman's cries of pain drifted through the cracked windows. Sandy kept her foot on the brake as they rolled adjacent to her.

"We're here to help!" she called.

Without warning, the woman turned toward them, her hair falling from her face and her cries turning to moans. She looked at them with crazed, black eyes. She was infected. Her mouth turned into a snarl and her teeth snapped viciously. It looked like she'd been there awhile.

Sandy froze in terror as she read a message that had been spray painted across the woman's tattered shirt: *"Hell is here."*

29

REGINALD WALKED FASTER AS HE reached the log cabin. Several windows on the cabin had been smashed out, leaving shards of glass stuck to the pane. He got close enough to see the front door hanging open.

He rounded the corner, aiming his pistol and his rifle. No one greeted him or stopped him. Other than the creature he'd killed outside, he hadn't seen anything else wandering nearby. He crept toward the cabin entrance until he felt secure that no one was inside. Then he stepped through the threshold, avoiding piles of clothing and supplies that had been smashed and raided. Several bags of snacks were scattered on the ground. An empty bottle of water lay on the floor, as if to taunt him. Reginald swore at the reminder of how thirsty he was. He wouldn't drink from the bottle, even though he saw several drops inside. He wouldn't be foolish enough to infect himself. He scanned the rest of the room, finding a mattress without sheets and a few tipped over chairs. A wave of tiredness crept over him. Reginald blinked, fighting the urge to lie down.

He needed rest.

But he needed to get to the lumberyard first.

He turned and faced the door again, noticing a few glimmers of color through the trees. He swung his rifle in their direction, his heart racing, until he realized the objects were merely clothing hung up to dry. The garments looked like they belonged to another cabin.

He'd check the rest of the area first before returning to the road.

Reginald took a step forward, stumbling as a wave of exhaustion swept over him. He paused. His face and shirt were damp from sweat. His limbs were spongy. Regardless of what his plans were, he needed to rest for a moment.

Reginald walked over to the cabin door, but instead of going through it, he shut it. Thankfully, the lock was intact. He staggered backward and lay on the bed, aiming his gun at the door and convincing himself that if anyone came at him, he'd hear them.

He'd hear them, and then he'd...

Reginald passed out.

30

A MEEK VOICE FROM THE BACKSEAT made Sandy turn her eyes to the rearview. Anabel was whispering something to her mother. A minute later Marcia spoke up.

"Anabel has to use the bathroom," Marcia said. Her tone was almost apologetic.

"I'm sorry," Anabel added quietly.

"Don't worry about it." Sandy smiled through her nervousness. She looked at Simon, who was scanning the road. "Do you think it's safe? Or should we go farther?"

Since passing the infected woman on the tree, they'd seen no further signs of danger, or any survivors. But that didn't dispel her unease.

Simon surveyed the trees. "I see a turnoff up ahead. Let's try it."

Sandy was wary as she pulled into the beaten, gravel-covered roadway, but she didn't see any signs of life. Trees flecked the road on either side. She took the turn slowly, curving through some trees to get out of view of the road, driving only far enough to conceal them and turn the minivan around.

"I'll step out first and make sure the area is clear," Simon said, carrying his rifle.

"Maybe we should all go," Hector suggested. "I'm not sure when we'll get another chance."

"Not a bad idea. Give me a minute."

Simon stepped out and looked around. After a few seconds, he motioned for the occupants to join him. Marcia, Hector, and Anabel hurried behind a nearby tree. Sandy kept her eyes on their surroundings, as if the forest might unleash a cavalcade of creatures. But it was empty. After using the bathroom, Sandy returned and stood next to Simon while Hector and Marcia finished up with Anabel.

"We've probably only driven a few miles," Simon said, glancing at the atlas page.

"I'm afraid to drive too fast," Sandy remarked.

"Of course. Some of the turns are sharp."

"What do the notes say?"

"They give landmarks, but they're a little vague."

"Hopefully we'll be able to follow them when we get there."

Sandy flexed her hands and looked at the deserted woods. The quiet was refreshing after spending days in the city, with only the hungry groans of the creatures to keep her company.

"This beats St. Matthews," she said as the cool wind rustled her hair.

"In a lot of ways, yes," Simon agreed. "But I'm still worried about what might be out there."

Sandy looked over at the rusted minivan behind them. Her fear had been that the vehicle would die, leaving them stranded. Thankfully it had been reliable. The light wind ceased, allowing the rustling trees to settle.

When they did, Sandy noticed another noise. Footsteps bled through the trees.

"Do you hear that?" she hissed.

"What?" Simon asked.

Sandy cocked her head. "Someone's coming."

She looked behind them, trying to grab Hector, Marcia, and Anabel's attention. They weren't looking.

"Over there," Simon whispered, pulling her attention to a patch of trees diagonal to them. His face grew fearful with alarm. "I hear it now."

Sandy aimed her gun at the empty patch of woods, watching a few leaves drift to the ground. The footsteps were getting closer. Sandy's eyes flicked to the minivan. They were close enough that they could get back inside easily, if they needed to, but they'd have to wait for Hector and his family. She turned and caught Hector's eyes as he emerged from behind the tree. She gestured with her pistol at the opposite side of the woods. Hector, Marcia, and Anabel scurried over toward Simon and Sandy.

They were halfway to the minivan when a tattered, bedraggled woman emerged from the forest. Her face was pale with fear as she yelled, "Help!"

31

THE WOMAN'S GRAY HAIR SWAYED over her shoulders as she yelled for assistance. Her face was fearful and confused.

"Stay back!" Simon warned her, aiming his rifle. "Hector, get your family in the car!"

Hector and his family got into the minivan. Sandy kept her gun trained. The appearance of the woman—in the middle of the woods, far from others—was enough to shake any comfort she had. The woman halted twenty yards away from them. Judging by her weathered skin and wrinkles, she was in her late sixties. Her dress was ripped and stained. She held up her hands in a placating gesture.

"Please don't shoot!" she pleaded. "My husband needs help!"

Sandy looked past the woman, as if her appearance might be distracting them from some other danger.

"Please, I know how hard it is to trust someone—believe me, I do. What else can I say to convince you I'm not lying?"

"Are you alone?" Simon asked, making it clear he didn't believe her.

"Yes! I left my husband behind. He's too injured to travel."

"Where is he?" Simon asked.

"He's in an RV down the woods," she said, gesturing behind her. "I've been hiding here, waiting for someone to come. I'm not sure what to do!"

Simon eyed her with doubt. "And you think we can help you?"

"Some people took our car and everything we had. Harold tried to stand up to them, but they stabbed him before they left." The woman watched Sandy and the others fearfully, as if they might do the same to her. "I have nothing left to lose. That's the only reason I came out. If you leave me, he'll die. And I won't last much longer without food and water."

Sandy and Simon watched the woman.

"When did this happen?"

"Yesterday. I barely got Harold back to the RV. He's bleeding pretty badly."

"Are you armed?" Simon asked.

"No," the woman smoothed out her dress to prove it. "They took everything, like I said."

Simon instructed her to turn around, but she seemed weaponless. After another glance around the woods, he lowered his gun. Sandy followed his lead. The woman approached cautiously, as if they might change their minds and shoot.

"Please don't leave me," she pleaded.

"Have you seen any of the creatures around?" Simon asked.

The woman shook her head. "Not in a while. But if you go far enough, you'll find them. They're everywhere."

"Is there anyone else up here?"

"Most of the people in the campsites have been infected or killed. We've been up here for a day with no food and water. That's when we found the RV. If we don't get help, we'll die either way."

Sandy blew a breath. The woman's report confirmed everything she'd feared. "Does the RV drive?"

"No. It's broken."

"What's your name?" she asked the woman.

"Donna."

Sandy introduced herself and the others. "How far did you say the RV is from here, Donna?"

Donna pulled herself together, turned, and pointed. "It's right through those trees, a few minutes away. It'd be quicker if we drove. But I don't blame you if you don't want me in your car. I can walk next to you, if you'd like."

Sandy looked at the minivan. She recalled the medical supplies they'd found at the elementary school. They might be able to help the injured man. They couldn't leave these people to die.

"We should take her," Hector piped up from inside the vehicle. "See if we can help her husband."

Sandy nodded and looked at Simon. After a brief, silent consensus, they waved the woman into the car.

Between the supplies and the new passenger, the minivan was crowded. Sandy and Simon reentered the front seats while Hector, Marcia, Anabel, and Donna squeezed in the back. Donna directed Sandy down the road.

"Keep going," she said. "You can't miss it. It's the only RV here. I haven't seen any other buildings or any other vehicles, but I didn't want to leave Harold too long."

"You said the RV doesn't run?" Sandy asked.

"No," Donna said. "We tried starting it, but it wouldn't even turn over. It looks like it was abandoned a while ago. If it drove, I'd take it for help. Even though I doubt I'd find any."

Sandy watched their surroundings as thick trees bordered either side of the road. A few picnic tables were chained to the trees, garbage bins knocked over next to them. Sandy saw a stiff, decaying body a few feet in the woods.

"Everyone else must've left when things started getting bad," Donna explained. "I haven't seen the men who robbed us. They must be long gone."

"I understand."

While they were driving, Donna continued her story. "Harold and I were taking a road trip before all this started. We were going from Albuquerque to St. Matthews. Harold had just retired. This was supposed to be our romantic getaway." Donna shook her head as tears welled in her eyes. "And then this happened. We've been fighting off those things for days, looking for help everywhere. When we finally saw a car, we pulled in. And then the people we met robbed us."

"You said Harold was stabbed?" Sandy asked.

"Yes. Yesterday. He's been getting worse and worse. I've tried to do what I can for him, but he's not responding." Donna broke into a gasping sob and covered her face with her hands as the gravity of her situation hit her.

They drove for a few minutes, crunching over gravel, looking for the RV. Simon kept his rifle in his hands as he surveyed the woods. They passed by several more spray-painted, unreadable signs until they reached a straightaway.

"Over there!" Donna spoke up, gesturing toward a dirt trail.

True to her word, a white RV sat at the end.

Sandy turned off the gravel road and onto the dirt. The people in the backseat tensed and sat forward. The minivan fought with the bumps in the road as they tried to get a better look at the vehicle. The RV was dingy, surrounded by picnic tables and a fire pit that had long since burned out. It was parked perpendicular to the dirt road. The front of it looked like a truck—the driver's and passenger's seats were inside. It was about thirty-five feet long. Movement from the side of it drew their attention. A person had appeared from around the back.

Simon aimed his rifle at Donna. "Who the hell's that?" he asked, staring back at her, as if she might've lured them into a trap.

"I don't know!" Donna said frantically. "Harold and I are alone, I swear!"

They watched the person walk down the side of the RV, rapping on the exterior, reaching for the windows. It didn't take them long to determine it was a creature. The creature had short, cropped hair, and it moaned as it pawed at the panes. Sandy's heart sank as another creature with long hair joined it. The things moved down the side of the RV, scraping and banging as if they knew someone was inside.

Sandy stopped a hundred yards away and appraised the scene.

"Harold's in there!" Donna whispered urgently. "He won't be able to defend himself, if they get in!"

Simon looked from the creatures to the people in the minivan. "If what you said is true, there are certainly more creatures in the area. Shooting them will draw others."

"Or people like the ones who robbed you," Sandy agreed.

"Let's take care of them quietly," Simon said. "Is the door to the RV locked?"

"Yes," Donna said.

"That'll buy us some time."

"I have the key." Donna pulled a key from her shoe.

Simon looked into the backseat. "Why don't the rest of you stay here while Sandy and I get out."

"No. I'm going," Hector said.

"Stay here with your family," Simon told him. "Keep them safe."

Hector shook his head. "Not this time. I want to do this."

"Hector—" Marcia started.

"I've sat out long enough, Marcia. I want to help. I want to pull my weight."

His tone overrode argument. The others traded apprehensive looks with Hector as he shuffled seats, getting out. Sandy left the engine running and joined Hector outside. They shut their doors with care, creeping through a few tall pines and getting farther away from the vehicle, approaching the creatures. Sandy clutched her knife and looked at Hector.

"There are only two of them," she said in a whisper. "We should be able to take care of them without much noise."

Hector nodded. "Okay."

They ducked behind a thick tree within twenty yards of the RV. The creatures didn't seem to notice their arrival—the shorter-haired one angrily pounded one of the windows, while the long-haired thing smacked the wall in frustration. Hector watched Sandy with wide eyes as they prepared a next move. Sandy clenched the knife in her hand. The prospect of voluntarily facing one of the things was never a welcome thought, but they'd do what they had to.

"I'll take the one on the left," she whispered.

"I'll take the one on the right."

After a quick signal, Sandy stepped out from the RV and charged, Hector behind her. Her shoes flew over a bed of pine needles and brush as she ran quickly and quietly. The creature she was aiming for didn't notice her until the last second, when it turned, exposing a set of dingy, stained teeth. She sunk the knife into its forehead before it could attack. She pulled the blade loose. The second creature was already coming at her, but Hector intercepted, cracking its skull with the barrel of his rifle. The thing fell against the RV, snarling and flailing. He hit it again with a blow to the head, watching it collapse. The creature sank into the pine needles, its eyes dull.

Sandy and Hector backed away from the downed creatures, their breath surging.

Sandy wiped her blade in the grass as she searched the forest for others. They stepped back from the RV as another moan piped up.

"Behind you!" she called to Hector. One of the creatures barreled out from the front of the RV and toward him. Dodging its groping hands, Hector flung an arm out and grabbed its shirt, pulling it off-balance and flinging it to the ground. The creature's blonde hair hung in tattered strips to its face and it snarled. Hector stomped its head with his boot, over and over, grinding its face into the ground until it stopped moving. When he was finished, he bent down, gasping for breath.

"That'll wake you up," he said as he made a face.

They remained in place for several seconds, listening to the keen of the wind through the trees. The attack seemed over. Sandy turned her attention to the curtained windows of the RV, expecting to find a grateful survivor peering at them through the panes, but the RV was lifeless. They checked all sides for more creatures, but found nothing else.

"Let's get back to the others," Hector said quietly. "Then we'll go inside."

32

ANDY, HECTOR, SIMON, MARCIA, ANABEL and Donna stood by the side entrance of the RV while Donna inserted the key. The door was located toward the middle, several feet behind the passenger's seat.

Before opening the door, Donna called quietly, "It's me, Harold! Everything's okay!"

She waited for an answer. When she didn't receive one, she gave the others a worried glance and opened the door. Sandy felt a surge of fear as she recalled other times she'd entered a room or a building, unwittingly rousing a group of creatures. She knew the door had been locked. And the RV didn't appear to have been compromised.

Still...

A whiff of something awful floated out to them. Sandy covered her mouth and nose at the recognizable odor of blood. She watched as Donna mounted the stairs, disappearing into the dark interior. When she'd reached the landing, Donna turned and waved them up.

"It's okay," she whispered. "Harold's in here."

Despite Donna's reassurances, Sandy and Simon crept up the stairs cautiously, wielding their guns in anticipation of an attack.

New odors washed over Sandy as she reached the landing. She smelled rotten food, mold, and people's sweat. She envisioned Donna and Harold holed up in the RV, afraid to leave, trapped with the remnants of the people who used to live there. She'd been in similar situations in St. Matthews. They were never ideal.

As her eyes adjusted to the dark, she saw a couch, an eating area, and several curtained windows on the right-hand wall. A wall of cabinets and appliances—including a stove and a mounted television—were on the left. The room was dark. She drew her attention toward the back of the RV. Past a small section in the middle, which seemed to contain a bathroom, she saw a bed with a man in it. He wasn't moving.

Donna gasped as ran toward the back of the RV and took his side.

"Harold?" she called frantically. "Harold! Please talk to me!" Donna wailed and knelt by her husband, frantically trying to rouse him, but he didn't stir.

Sandy and Simon reached her side, carrying the medical supplies they'd brought from the minivan, trying to get a closer look, while Hector, Marcia, and Anabel hung by the side door.

Donna pressed her fingers to his neck. "He has no pulse!" She looked at them, as if someone might be playing a cruel trick on her.

"See if he's breathing," Sandy tried, leaning down next to him. Her hope was to hear a thin

T.W. Piperbrook

rasp, something to give them hope. The man was lifeless.

"Can we open the curtains?" Hector asked.

"Yes," Donna said, reaching over the bed and drawing up a curtain. "I was keeping them closed to avoid notice."

The new light revealed a man much older than sixty. Or maybe it was the result of his wounded condition. He wasn't moving. He wasn't speaking. His eyes were dim and sightless, and he stared at a spot on the ceiling, his lips blue. His shirt was soaked with blood, and several towels were laid over him, pressed over what must be the wound in his stomach.

Sandy lowered the medical supplies as she and the others realized the man was past saving.

"I'm sorry," Sandy said.

"No!" Donna said, looking around wildly. She shook Harold, as if he might wake up and speak with her, but the man was silent and still. "Harold, please wake up!"

Sandy, Simon, and Hector watched her with a grave expression. Donna's insistent words segued into mournful moans as she realized what the others already had. Harold was dead. Looking behind her, Sandy saw Marcia leading Anabel out the side door of the RV, forcing the girl to look away.

Sandy lowered her head, praying Harold's death was the last casualty she'd have to witness.

"We'd been waiting for years to travel," Donna said, drying her tears as Sandy sat next to her on the couch. "I can't believe this. He wanted to show me the world. And now that will never happen."

"I'm sorry," Sandy said, patting the woman's knee.

Simon and Hector covered up the body with a sheet while Marcia and Anabel waited outside.

Sensing Donna needed distraction, Sandy asked, "He retired recently?"

"Yes. He was a travel agent for forty years," Donna said, smiling through her tears. "You'd think we would've gotten out more. But we only got to see a few places he booked trips to. He was so busy working, you know. Things got harder with the Internet. But Harold never gave up. That's how he was. He was dedicated to his business; he ran it for forty years. A few months ago, he retired and told me he'd take me around the world. He was going to make up for all the time we'd lost."

"He sounds like a hardworking person."

Donna exhaled a shuddering breath. "He was. I just wish I'd been able to help him."

"You did your best," Sandy affirmed. "That's all any of us can do."

"I tried moving him a few times, hoping we could go somewhere and find help. But he wasn't up for it. If those things came, or those men returned, they would've run us down, especially in his condition."

Sandy lowered her head. The guilt Donna was feeling reminded her of the guilt she felt for Ben. She couldn't count how many times she'd relived her brother's last moments, wishing that things had gone differently.

Hector and Simon joined Sandy and Donna on the couch, uttering condolences. Donna thanked them. The smell in the RV seemed to be getting worse, and Sandy had the pressing urge to get out. She suddenly felt trapped, claustrophobic. She stood, looking back at the body lying on the bed. Donna followed her gaze.

"Can we bury him?" Donna asked numbly.

After a pause, Simon said, "We have two shovels in the trunk."

"I'll help dig," Hector offered.

33

T HEY LOCATED A SPOT IN the woods a hundred yards from the RV where the dirt was soft enough to unearth. Using the shovels they'd taken from the elementary school, Simon and Hector scooped dirt into a pile. Marcia and Anabel remained on the other side of the RV, away from the gory scene. Sandy comforted Donna, trying to remain stoic as she watched Harold's motionless body.

Sweat rolled down Simon's forehead. Neither he nor Hector spoke as they finished digging, wiping sweat from their brows and laying their shovels on the forest floor. When they were finished, they took hold of Harold's arms and legs and gently placed him in the makeshift grave. They paused, listening to the chirping birds and watching a swooping hawk search for prey. Sunlight poured through the thick boughs of the overhanging trees.

Donna knelt down next to Harold, but couldn't seem to manage any words.

"I'll say a prayer, if you'd like," Simon offered, quietly.

Donna nodded, wiping her eyes. Simon recited a prayer that sounded familiar, but she couldn't be sure. Sandy barely registered the meaning of those phrases, and yet they somehow gave her a measure of comfort. When Simon finished, he leaned on his shovel and watched Donna.

"Take all the time you need," he said quietly as he turned away. "We'll cover him when you're done."

Donna cried quietly for a few minutes on her knees. She dabbed at the tears on her face, which seemed never-ending. Finally, her expression grew hard. "I hope the bastards who did this rot in hell." She reached out for Simon's shovel. "I need to do this."

Simon nodded and gave it to her. Donna scooped dirt over her husband while the others watched, sweating, as if the exertion might distract her from her grief. When she was finished, she patted the ground and stepped back. Her face softened into a wave of emotion. She knelt back down.

"You were my best friend for forty-five years, Harold. I couldn't have asked for a better soul mate. I hope you rest in peace. Wherever you are, I'm sure it's better than here."

Before she could break down again, Donna turned and walked away.

Sandy, Hector, and Simon followed Donna through the trees, sympathy on their faces. The RV stood silent and still, a monument to Harold. The forest had turned preternaturally quiet, as if the animals were respectfully mourning his death. Sandy looked above them. Was God watching them, or had He already forsaken them? She didn't know what to believe anymore. She'd seen too much death.

She thought back to the families she'd seen in the beginning of the infection, sticking together as the carnage unfolded around them. She'd seen people fall, people carried, and people left behind. Inevitably, families had been separated.

The death of Donna's husband was a grim reminder of that.

They walked in silence, their footsteps the only sound as they approached the RV. Donna's occasional sniffle broke the quiet. They were halfway to the RV when Sandy realized the quiet was deeper than it should've been.

Something was missing.

"Where are Marcia and Anabel?" she asked.

"Marcia?" Hector called, frowning as he increased his pace.

Sandy, Simon, and Donna joined in, calling them.

"Marcia? Anabel?"

Past the RV, the minivan sat on the dirt road, idle and empty. Sandy, Hector, and Simon raised their guns. The forest suddenly felt menacing and sinister, as if it'd come to life and snatched Marcia and Anabel away. They'd been right on the other side of the RV a few moments ago. Sandy was sure of it. She'd heard them. At least, she thought she had.

Hector called out again with no response. They were within twenty yards of the RV, walking faster. Marcia had a gun. If something had happened, they would've heard it.

When they rounded the corner, they saw the reason for the silence. Marcia stood trembling on the other side of the RV, her hands raised, her gun on the ground.

Thirty feet away from her, staring at them with violent, angry eyes, Reginald pointed a gun at the side of Anabel's head and shouted, "Take a step and I blow her head off!"

PART THREE
CLING TO THE EDGE

34

"LET MY DAUGHTER GO!" HECTOR cried, prompting Reginald to tighten his grip around Anabel's neck and take a step backward with her.

Marcia sobbed and held up her hands. "Please!"

Sandy, Simon, and Hector lowered their guns, terrified they'd make a wrong move that would cause the little girl's death. Donna gasped and watched Reginald. Reginald's eyes blazed as he looked over all of them. He looked confused, angry. His hands shook. In one, he held a pistol to Anabel's temple. In the other, he held a rifle, his arm snaked around the little girl's neck. His face was cut and scratched, as if he'd been involved in a struggle or a fight.

Sandy tried to determine how things had gone so wrong, so quickly. Where had Reginald come from? Why was he here? There wasn't time to speculate.

"Everyone put your guns on the ground! Now!" he snarled.

Sandy bent down and set her pistol on the ground. Out of the corner of her eye, she saw Simon and Hector doing the same. They backed away from the weapons.

"Get your hands on the RV!"

With Anabel's life at stake, they had no choice but to comply. Sandy walked over and placed her hands on the vehicle's exterior, fearful that the next sound she heard would be a bullet. She kept her eyes on the RV and said a silent prayer. Behind her, she heard Reginald bend down and pick up the guns. He backed up, keeping a tight grip on Anabel, collecting them in a pile by his feet.

"Who has the keys to the van?" he demanded.

After a second of silence, Sandy said, "I do." She pulled them slowly from her pocket and tossed them behind her. She listened to Reginald slide them backward with his foot. Anabel whimpered as Reginald bent down and grabbed them from the dirt.

"Listen, this doesn't have to go any further," Hector said.

"The hell it doesn't," Reginald snarled, looking at each of them. "I knew I couldn't trust you. You left the lumberyard. You took the supplies and you left."

The group remained silent. After a brief pause, Simon said calmly, "The lumberyard was overrun by those things."

"Bullshit," Reginald snarled. "You took everything and you left."

"That's not the way it happened. If you'll listen, I'll explain."

"Shut up." Reginald fell quiet for a moment,

seeming to notice Donna for the first time. "Who's this?"

"They helped me," Donna spoke up, her voice wavering as she turned to look over her shoulder. "My husband died. They helped me bury him."

Sandy took a peek back at Reginald. His face was expressionless, as if he didn't register emotion. His gaze drifted back to the others.

"Where are Billy and Tom?" Simon asked.

A flicker of confusion went through Reginald's face as he recalled something. "They're dead."

"What happened to them?"

"Does it matter? Now, where is it?"

Simon was unable to hide his confusion. "Where's what?"

Reginald squeezed Anabel's neck harder, eliciting a cry of pain. "Where is it?" he shouted. "I know you took it!"

"Please!" Sandy said. "If you're looking for the food and water, it's in the minivan. You can take all of it, if you need to, but let Anabel go."

"That's not what I mean, and you know it!" Reginald shouted, growing enraged.

Somewhere in the distant trees, an animal skittered to safety, causing Reginald to turn wildly in all directions. He blinked a line of sweat from his eyes and adjusted his grip on Anabel. He stared at the minivan. For a moment, Sandy considered running at him, grabbing the gun, and wrenching Anabel from his arms. But the idea was as foolish as it was impossible.

She looked down at her waist, catching sight of the knife protruding from her pants. The others had knives, too, but they'd be no match for a gun. In any case, it didn't look like Reginald hadn't noticed. She hoped it stayed that way.

"Turn around!" Reginald yelled, noticing Sandy peering over her shoulder.

"Whatever you're looking for, we'll help you find it," Hector said.

"Keep your backs turned, I said!"

Reginald pulled Anabel back and forth to the van, bringing the weapons with him. "I'll find what I'm looking for myself. You better hope it's in there, for the little girl's sake."

"Please!" Marcia called over her shoulder.

Reginald ignored her. He opened the van and transferred the weapons from the ground to the passenger's seat. Then he started rummaging through the vehicle's interior. His frustration found its way into curses as he didn't find what he was looking for. Sandy looked desperately at Hector, Marcia, Donna, and Simon, hoping someone might have a desperate solution. She glanced at her knife again.

"If we try anything, he'll kill us," Hector replied, noticing Sandy's gaze.

"Don't tempt him. Please," Marcia added.

"Does anyone know what he's looking for?" Simon asked.

They shook their heads.

Without warning, Donna seemed to decide on something, turning around and taking a step.

"Donna, where are you going?" Marcia hissed.

Donna ignored her. "You don't need to do this," Donna called over to Reginald, holding her hands in the air and walking toward the minivan. "There's no need for violence."

"Stay the fuck back!" Reginald warned. Sandy looked over her shoulder, her heart thrumming in her chest.

"I just lost my husband. We don't need to put another family through that," Donna continued. "These are good people."

"Donna, please!" Marcia whispered. "Get back here!"

Donna continued, "My husband died because a group of violent men. They took everything we had. They stabbed Harold. I couldn't take care of him, and he died. That's when these people stopped to help me. If they hadn't, I might've died up here, too."

Reginald raised his gun. "Why do you think I give a shit about your husband? And why do you think I give a shit about you?"

"Donna!" Marcia cried. "Please get back here!"

Reginald fired.

Donna screamed in pain as a bullet struck her in the leg, dropping her to the ground. The world descended into chaos as people turned, pleaded, and tried to help her up. Reginald warned them to stay back. He waved his guns until they scurried back to the RV.

"Get your hands on the wall!"

Reginald walked over and tried to force Donna to stand, but she only screamed in pain, holding her leg.

"Where is it?" he shouted at all of them, growing even more infuriated.

"We don't know!" Marcia said earnestly. "If you let us know what you're looking for, we can help you!"

The campsite went quiet except for the frantic breathing of the people against the RV and Donna's sobbing. For a moment, Sandy was sure Reginald would fire at each of them in turn, ending all their lives.

Without a word, he strode back to the minivan.

A cold pit grew in Sandy's stomach. Sandy caught Marcia's eyes, which were wide and coated with fear. For a second time, she considered running at Reginald with her knife.

"As soon as he doesn't find what he's looking for, he's going to kill her!" Hector whispered.

Reginald's cursing and swearing floated over from the minivan as he rifled through the interior. Sandy gave a cautious glance over her shoulder. She saw him searching under the seats, checking the glove compartment, keeping Anabel close enough to harm her if they tried anything.

Donna had settled into a low wail of pain as she clutched her leg. Hopelessness and desperation washed over Sandy. She looked around, thinking she'd see another vehicle—Reginald's—but she saw nothing but forest.

Each bang from the minivan brought Reginald closer to a rage that they couldn't calm. After a few more minutes of searching, he slammed the door and dragged Anabel back over to the RV. This time he planted himself behind Simon, placing a gun to the back of his head.

"I'm done with the bullshit. You took my shit, traitor," he said, giving no room for argument. "You found what I had in the lumberyard, and you took it. I'm going to give you one chance to tell me where it is, and then I'm going to shoot you. And then I'll shoot each one of you until someone answers."

Simon remained quiet. Sandy watched Simon's expression as he stood next to her. The look of fear and uncertainty in his eyes showed that he was just as clueless as the rest of them. He opened his mouth, preparing what might be the last response of his life.

Something moved behind Reginald.

It was Donna.

35

ONNA BASHED INTO REGINALD'S LEGS with a feral rage, sending him off balance enough to make him let go of his rifle. Anabel screamed and scurried away. Donna bit Reginald's leg as he fought to stay upright.

"Let go of me, you bitch!"

Donna hung on. Reginald raised his pistol, trying to shoot her, but she clawed his arms, batting it away. At the same time, Sandy dove for Reginald's dropped rifle while Simon jumped at Reginald. Suddenly Donna was crawling away, and Simon was fighting for the pistol.

"Get Anabel in the RV!" Sandy yelled at Hector and Marcia.

They raced for the RV, ushering their daughter to safety. The pistol swung wildly in all directions as Simon and Reginald fought for it. Sandy tried aiming the rifle at Reginald, but couldn't get off a shot in the commotion.

The pistol discharged. Birds took flight in the forest as a bullet screamed through the trees. Sandy repeatedly tried to get close, but each time, a swinging arm blocked her from intercepting. Blood ran from Reginald's nose as he fought and kicked. Simon grunted as he tried to overpower him. The gun went off again. Suddenly Simon and Reginald were on the ground, fighting. Sandy spun to check on Donna. She was no longer crawling.

One of the bullets had struck her in the side of the head. Blood puddled from a bullet wound, and she lay perfectly still on her stomach.

"No!" Sandy screamed, racing over to the woman.

Donna was motionless, her mouth open in a surprised grimace of death. Sandy spun and pointed the rifle at the battling men, her body coursing with adrenaline and fear. It looked like Simon had gotten the upper hand. He pinned one of Reginald's arms—the one with the pistol— above his head, and he pummeled him in the face. Reginald cried out and spat blood. Simon ripped the gun free. Reginald made one last lunge, taking Simon by surprise and knocking it from his hands. The pistol skittered underneath the RV.

And then Reginald was on his feet and running.

Simon screamed his name, chasing him into the woods.

"Simon! Where are you going?" Sandy yelled after him.

"He has the keys!" Simon called as he pursued Reginald.

Before she could make a decision as to whether to follow, they disappeared into the thick brush. Commotion drew Sandy's attention to the forest in the opposite direction. A group of four creatures had emerged, sprinting toward the RV.

Sandy's heart pounded as she aimed the rifle, hoping to cut some of them off. She fired. Her aim was good enough to wound one of them, and it toppled sideways. She fired several more times, catching another in the chest, causing it to fall on its face. Two others charged, swiping the air as they anticipated consuming her. Sandy managed to hit another in the head before the remaining creature was too close to shoot. She swung the butt of the rifle, bashing it in the face as it approached, cracking out a few of its already-chipped teeth. The creature snarled and fell to one knee. She struck it again, knocking it to the ground, then hovered over it and finished it off with a blow to the skull.

She ran over to the wounded creatures, yanking out her knife and finishing them off. Looking up, she saw more creatures emerging from the forest.

"Simon!" she yelled at the empty forest.

There was no sign of the fleeing men.

More hisses forced her to spin and assess the situation. The creatures were flooding from all directions, drawn by the noise. She looked at the RV, envisioning Hector, Marcia, and Anabel inside, alone and unarmed. Making a decision, Sandy ran to the minivan to collect the weapons Reginald had stashed there. She hoped she had enough time.

She ripped open the door, grabbing what she could before panic made her run. She'd managed to get another pistol and a rifle, adding to the one rifle she had. She left one rifle behind. The creatures were too close to delay any longer.

Sandy sprinted past Donna's lifeless body. There was no time to mourn.

Soon she was pounding on the RV door, screaming Hector, Marcia, and Anabel's names as they let her inside.

36

As the trees thickened, Simon questioned what he was doing. The adrenaline and the commotion—and the fact that Reginald had the keys—had prompted him to run after him, but now he questioned that judgment. Groans emanated from the forest. The creatures were everywhere. The keys to the minivan would be useless without the means to get the others inside and drive it.

He turned, thinking of heading back, when he caught sight of creature in a tattered jacket, coming swiftly in his direction. He spun and kept running. Reginald stumbled through the trees, glancing over his shoulder at Simon. His face was lined with sweat and blood. Simon recalled what he'd seen before taking off after Reginald. Donna had been shot in the struggle. It looked like she was dead. That knowledge gave Simon a surge of anger. He let that drive him as he kept moving.

Even though his lungs were burning, Simon was in decent shape. In Tucson, he'd worked construction, and although the gigs had been sporadic, he'd kept himself active. He increased pace and narrowed the gap with Reginald. Looking behind him, he noticed he'd lost the creature behind him. He gritted his teeth and pushed on.

Rounding a tree, he saw Reginald slowing down in the distance. Reginald was hovering next to a thick tree trunk for balance, looking back at Simon, a frightened expression in his eyes. For a moment, Simon thought that Reginald was going to give up. *Or maybe he's planning something.* Simon patted his pockets. Reginald had taken their guns, but he hadn't noticed their knives. That fact might help Simon. He pulled out the blade, keeping it low so Reginald wouldn't see it.

"Reginald!" he called, holding the man's gaze.

Just when Simon thought he might catch up, Reginald ran at full speed again, dipping around a few trees and out of sight. Simon frowned as he tried to decipher where he'd gone. The creatures were gaining ground again. The crashes and wails behind him were signals that Simon needed to keep moving, whether he pursued Reginald or not.

Simon kept going, keeping his eye on the forest for places that Reginald might hide and attack him. He saw no sign of the panting, bloodied man. If he could catch sight of him, at least he'd—

Simon slid.

One minute he was running, the next he was barreling down a ravine, fighting for balance, groping at rocks and dirt. Brush and weeds snagged his T-shirt and pants, sending spears of pain through him as he fell. He fought to control

T.W. Piperbrook

his descent, catching hold of several jutting branches, losing hold of them almost as soon as he grasped them. His knife slipped from his hand. Simon cried out as he struck a thin tree and tumbled forward onto his stomach. And then he was at the bottom, his body catching up to the toll of pain. His breath was gone. Simon squinted from the glare of the sun as he landed, trying to catch his bearings. The wind blew, carrying the groans of the creatures from somewhere above him.

He wasn't safe.

He pushed off the ground, forcing himself through the aches and wounds, and found uneasy purchase. He looked for his knife, but it was lost in a sea of sliding sand and gravel, buried in the side of the ravine somewhere. He wouldn't find it without effort. He took a staggering step forward and caught his breath.

He didn't notice Reginald until he was already lunging, Simon's knife in his hand.

37

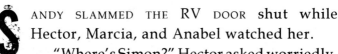

ANDY SLAMMED THE RV DOOR shut while Hector, Marcia, and Anabel watched her.

"Where's Simon?" Hector asked worriedly.

"He went after Reginald. He was trying to get the keys to the van."

"Dammit." Hector shook his head. "He'll never make it back. Those things are everywhere."

"We're going to have to try and fight them off," Sandy said. Even as she said the words, she felt a pit of dread in her stomach that she couldn't shake. She'd seen what had happened when the creatures had surrounded others, and it never ended well.

She passed Hector and Marcia the weapons she'd been able to grab. Hector carried a rifle while Marcia carried the pistol, and Sandy kept Reginald's rifle. Footsteps shook the earth as the creatures flew through the campground, moaning and screeching, getting closer to the RV.

"Is there anywhere we can put Anabel?"

"There's a bathroom in the middle of the RV," Marcia said, terror on her face.

Sandy spun as she assessed the vehicle. The RV was much smaller now that she was trying to determine its defensibility. Small windows surrounded the bed in the back. The right-hand wall was solid and lined with cabinets, so that was relatively secure. The left-hand side worried her. The windows above the couch and the small eating area were large enough for the creatures to break and gain access. The front windshield was covered with a sun blinder, which might protect them from the infected trying to peer inside, but did nothing to reinforce the glass. The windows next to the driver and passenger's seats were also breakable.

If only this damn thing drove.

Sandy walked over to one of the curtained windows and slid her finger between the fabric and the glass, peering out. The view provided her with more terror than relief.

"How many are out there?" Hector asked her.

"Too many," Sandy said in a panic. "They're approaching from all sides."

They stepped back as they listened to the creatures shrieking, assuming positions in the middle of the RV. Sandy wondered if Hector was harboring the same hope that she was: that somehow, the creatures would change direction and leave them alone. A pair of pounding hands shattered that hope. Nails slid down the RV. Another set of hands smacked the side. Sandy and Hector huddled close, as if the creatures might burst through the walls and grab them.

"We should block the side door," Sandy said, pointing at the entrance they'd come through.

"Is the couch bolted down?" Hector asked.

"I'm not sure. Let's try it."

They took either end of the couch, grunting as they pulled. Thankfully, the couch wasn't secured, and they were able to slide it in front of the door. If the creatures got in, the couch wouldn't buy them much more than time.

"How about the table? Maybe we can prop that against the windows," Hector suggested, pointing to the eating area.

Sandy tried to move it. "It's bolted down."

A particularly loud screech made her jump. The RV groaned as one of the creatures rammed against the side. A few more creatures followed suit. Sandy heard several creatures pounding at the windows near the bed in back. Thankfully, those windows were small enough that she didn't think they could get through that way. But that didn't make her feel any better. Sandy felt like she was submerged in some underground vessel that was crashing into a rocky reef, infected tearing at the hull.

One of the creature's hands slapped the glass of the passenger's side window. She saw a twisted, infected face appear against the pane, looking in at them. They remained still as it searched from left to right. Once it found a way in, it'd lead others.

Marcia rejoined them as they stood in the middle of the RV, spinning and watching each noise as they pointed their guns, waiting for the moment when the vehicle was breached.

38

IMON LEAPT TO THE SIDE, barely avoiding a slice from Reginald's knife. Reginald's face twisted in violent rage as he swung at Simon. The aches and pains in Simon's body were overridden by the primal knowledge that if he didn't move, he'd die. He backed away, trying to keep his balance on the rocky, sandy slope and get clear of a swing. Behind Reginald were thick trees. Getting around Reginald wasn't an option, at the moment. Going backwards was a recipe for death.

Simon avoided another jab, throwing up his hands instinctively to stop the sharp blade. Without a gun or his knife, he was defenseless.

"Fucking traitor." Reginald's face was hard and unwavering. Sweat poured down his brow. Simon knew there would be no reasoning with the irrational, crazed man, but self-preservation urged him to try.

"We don't need to do this, Reginald!" Simon tried. "We can talk!"

Reginald's answer was another swing. Simon dodged.

"The lumberyard was overrun," Simon said.

"Those things ran through the gate. We were looking for you."

Another swing. Another dodge.

"Bullshit! You think I believe that? You took everything! You took my shit!"

"Reginald!"

"Shut the fuck up!" Reginald spat.

Reginald's face was unforgiving as he lunged again. Simon avoided the blow, but lost his footing. He fell to the ground, losing his breath as he landed hard on his back. A shimmer of pain ran through his spine as he tried to stand. Reginald hovered over him. Simon raised his forearms instinctively, trying to protect his face, catching the tip of Reginald's knife. He cried out as hot blood trickled down his forearm. He rolled, trying desperately to get away from his attacker. But Reginald was on his feet and quicker. Reginald jabbed the knife downwards at Simon's face. Simon barely avoided it. The blade embedded in the dirt.

Reginald pulled the knife out and dove at Simon.

Suddenly Simon was underneath Reginald, barely catching hold of Reginald's wrist as he tried to stab downward. He struggled to keep the blade at bay.

"Reginald, stop!" he managed, between gritted teeth.

Reginald's face was determined as he pushed the blade. Whether it was Simon's weakened condition, or Reginald's intense rage, Simon wasn't sure, but he was losing. He strained as sweat poured down his face. He'd faced death many times in the past week, but nothing like this.

Noise from upslope drew their attention. Reginald flicked his gaze upward. Stones rolled down the ravine, loosened by the creatures that were making their way down. Moans filled the air. Taking the opportunity, Simon kneed Reginald in the groin. Reginald cried out and tried to protect his body, but he was too late. Simon pushed him off but lost hold of the knife. Suddenly Simon was on the move, staggering away from the hill as the creature's groans filled the air.

He looked back to find Reginald scrambling to his feet with the knife, facing a handful of creatures that were sliding down the ravine, surrounding him.

39

"THEY'RE GOING TO GET IN!" Marcia cried frantically as she swiveled around the RV.

Sandy could no longer guess how many of the things were out there. She looked out of the nearest curtain, assessing the situation again. Innumerable pairs of hands pawed greedily at the side of the RV. Mottled faces and blood-caked, hungry mouths hung open when they saw her. A wave of helplessness washed over her as she let the curtain go. She'd fought the creatures plenty of times, but never this many, and never at once. Each bang on the windows was a reminder that they were in an oversized container that might as well be a human cage.

"If they get in, conserve your bullets," Sandy said, trying to think logically. She held up her knife. "Use your knives when you can."

Hector and Marcia nodded, pulling out their blades.

A window above the eating area shattered.

They cried out and stepped back as a hand wormed its way over the sill, then an elbow. A creature mustered its strength to get up and over. Luckily, the window was tall enough to make the thing struggle.

"I've got it!" yelled Hector as he raced toward the thing, stabbing its arm.

Blood spurted from the creature's new wound and it lost its grip and fell. Another took its place, scrambling and pulling harder, getting two arms over before Hector kicked its fingers, managing to send it tumbling. A writhing mass of others fought for its place, screeching and hissing. Another window shattered, and suddenly more creatures were clambering over the top of the eating area.

"Come on!" Sandy yelled to Marcia. "We have to help!"

They raced over and joined Hector, stabbing the things with their knives. Sandy did her best to stay away from open mouths and groping hands. She stepped back as a creature thrust its arm over the sill, trying to catch hold of her. Marcia darted in and stabbed the creature with her knife, knocking it back.

Sandy plunged her knife into creatures' heads and arms—whatever she saw first. She stabbed relentlessly, until her arm was sore and the creatures felt like they were one violent mass, bent on taking over the RV. A third window shattered. Sandy swiveled her attention to it. Marcia ran over to it, trying to stop a creature from getting in.

Marcia screamed. One moment she was defending the window, the next she was fighting to keep from going over the sill. A creature had caught hold of her hair, pulling. Marcia lost hold of her pistol, dropping it into a mound of creatures. She tried wrenching herself free, but the creature had too tight a grip.

"Marcia!" Hector screamed, grabbing Marcia's waist and trying to pull her backwards. More creatures mimicked the first creature's success, jumping up and snagging Marcia's hair. The creatures were like rabid animals, sensing weakness.

Sandy raised her pistol, running over to the window and shooting the first thing in the side, prompting it to let go and fall over the sill. It took a clump of Marcia's hair with it. The things seemed as if they were multiplying, climbing over one another to get to the screaming woman. Hector managed to pull Marcia backward and into the RV, but not without her losing another clump of hair. All at once the three of them were in the middle, watching the creatures snake their arms over the windowsills.

Marcia was red-faced. Tears were in her eyes as she nursed her bleeding, sore scalp. "I lost my gun," she said.

"There's too many," Hector breathed.

Sandy looked around the room for some miracle that would stop the creatures from coming in. But the only way to stop them was fighting them. With no other choice, she swung her pistol back toward the open windows and kept firing.

40

IMON RAN UNTIL HIS SIDES ached and he could no longer hear the moans of the creatures. Looking back over his shoulder, he'd lost sight of Reginald. Gunshots sounded deep in the distance in the opposite direction. He didn't need to see the source to know that it was his companions. He'd run into an area of deep forest, with tree trunks thicker than his body. Several creatures coursed through the distant trees, changing direction, heading toward the faraway noise. Simon kept low, avoiding being spotted.

He hoped the creatures fighting Reginald had taken care of him.

He deserved to die for what he'd done to Charlie and to Donna.

And for all Simon knew, what he'd done to Billy and Tom.

Son of a bitch.

He gritted his teeth as he tried to quell the aching in his body. The fight with Reginald and the fall down the hill had sapped his strength. He needed to keep going.

Simon snuck through oaks and pines, hiding behind the thick trunks when he needed to, heading in the general direction of the RV. He couldn't allow his friends to be killed the way his sister had been. The memory of Rebecca's dying, pained face still haunted him. Even after his efforts to save her, he'd been too late.

He couldn't have the deaths of Sandy, Hector, Marcia, and Anabel on his conscience, too. He hadn't realized it before, but he understood why he'd stayed with them now — they'd given him hope that there was something on the other side of this.

He let that thought drive him as he skirted through the trees, picking up speed as he ran for the RV.

He barely saw Reginald stepping out from behind the tree.

Pain lanced through Simon's left shoulder as he managed to turn, avoiding a knife in the back. He cried out, reflexively reaching for the blade embedded in his shoulder. Reginald was already attempting to pull it out. Simon spun and pushed the man away, thrusting him into a tree.

Reginald's face was marred with blood. His eyes darted wildly and his shirt hung off of him. Bite marks flecked his stomach. He ran at Simon, but Simon held up his hands, meeting him. Simon's shoulder screamed from the stuck blade, but there was no time to deal with the pain. There was only time to fight, to live.

Reginald shrieked in rage and clutched onto Simon. Simon threw him sideways. Reginald exhaled as the breath was knocked from him.

Simon cocked back his right arm and punched Reginald in the face. He punched him again, causing Reginald to cough and spit blood. Reginald skirted to the side. His eyes blazed as he watched the knife.

He lunged. Simon tried avoiding him, but Reginald caught the knife handle, twisting it. Flashes of light crossed Simon's eyes as he fought against the intense pain. He flung a fist, catching Reginald in the nose, bursting it open.

"You son of a bitch!" Reginald screamed.

He held his broken nose and stepped backward.

As Simon's vision cleared, he surveyed the area in which they were fighting. Branches stuck out at all angles from the trunks of fallen trees. Reginald had backed up next to one of them. Simon didn't wait for the right moment.

He charged, knocking into Reginald with all his weight, thinking of Charlie, and Donna, and his companions that were left behind in the RV. He thought of Reginald's threats to starve them, and his empty promises to keep them safe.

Dan had been right. So had Sandy.

Simon hurled Reginald backward and into the fallen tree. Reginald cried out as he landed on one of the severed, sharp branches, the pointed end coming through his stomach, spraying his blood all over Simon. Reginald looked from Simon to the wound, as if it might be some illusion.

And then Reginald's head slumped forward, his eyes staring blankly at the forest as they lost light.

41

S ANDY, HECTOR, AND MARCIA SHOT the creatures that were climbing over the windowsill. Every few seconds, a vicious face would appear, and they'd shoot it back, watching the thing plummet into a mob of others. They'd given up on using knives in favor of guns. It was too dangerous to get close to the creatures, with so many in close proximity.

The banging continued on all sides of the RV. Sandy feared the vehicle would start to sway, topple over, and pin them inside. The possibility was unlikely, but who knew what was possible anymore? A while ago, she was living a quiet, normal life, enjoying time with her brother.

Now she was engaged in a bitter struggle for her life.

Some of their shots connected, but others dinged off the interior of the RV. The world had become a chaotic combination of groans and gunfire. Sandy felt as if she'd descended into a hellish warzone, battling creatures that were closer to demons than humans. The smell of blood from Harold's body hung in the air, a reminder that Sandy and the others might join him soon. She had a quick thought of Simon, and wondered if he'd fared any better, but she didn't have time to think about it further. One of the creatures ripped away her attention.

Sandy aimed at a longhaired, scraggly creature that had gotten a leg up over the windowsill. Its boot was caked with dirt. Its face was stained with blood. She pulled the trigger, but missed. She fired again. Her gun clicked empty.

"Dammit! I'm out!" she yelled to the others.

Hector and Marcia moved to cover her while she fumbled to reload, tucking in a new magazine. She joined the others in blasting the things, watching as several more creatures toppled out of view. Once their ammunition was out, they'd have no choice but to fight in close quarters.

A particularly loud bang drew her attention to the front of the vehicle. She looked around, panicked. Had one of the creatures gotten in?

"Shit! Over there!" Hector yelled, pulling her attention to the front windshield. One of the creatures crawled over the glass. She could see its shadow through the visor. More creatures joined it. The windshield groaned underneath the creatures' boots and bare, bloodied feet. Several of them jumped up and down on the pane.

She looked around for something that might prevent the glass from caving, even though that was probably impossible.

The pane shattered.

Creatures poured through the pane and onto the front seats and the dashboard, oblivious to the fragments of glass that were cutting them. Their black eyes darted around the vehicle as they spotted Sandy, Hector, and Marcia. Sandy backpedaled, trying to gain distance while firing at them. The creatures clambered over the steering wheel, trampling the windshield protector. Sandy bumped into Marcia and Hector.

They fired as a single unit at the salivating, hissing infected. More creatures converged on the opening.

"Shit! I'm out of bullets!" Hector yelled.

He lowered his rifle and reached for spare ammunition as he screamed at the others to keep shooting.

Sandy looked right. The creatures were climbing over the windowsills. She looked straight ahead, where creatures crawled over the fallen bodies of the dead. She shared a look with Marcia that neither needed to interpret.

We'll never kill them all.

42

IMON'S ARM BURNED AS HE ran, but he didn't think any arteries or nerves were damaged, because he could move it. As soon as he'd been away from Reginald, he'd pulled out the knife, but now he questioned that decision. Blood leaked from the wound. He'd tied it up with a strip of his t-shirt, but that was only helping so much. He didn't have time to analyze it further.

He needed to get to the RV.

He patted his pocket, ensuring that the van keys he'd taken from Reginald were still there. He raced in the direction of the gunshots, which were still loud and prevalent enough to convince him that his friends were still alive. Simon heaved thick breaths as he ran through the forest, heading toward an incline that lead to a higher elevation. That was where the RV was. At least, he thought so.

He listened to gunfire echo through the forest, fearing it would stop and make him lose his way. His legs ached as he pushed himself up the incline, moving diagonally to cover more ground. The slope was rocky and peppered with shrubs and trees, but he used his good hand to hang on to them, helping him along. When he reached the top, he located the RV through the trees.

The creatures had surrounded the vehicle. Even from a distance, he saw the things crawling over the windshield and leaping up at the windows. The side windows had been smashed. He heard groans and stamping feet from inside. Simon ran toward the scene. His fear was that his friends would die the same way so many others had—trapped in a place they thought was safe, which had turned into a tomb.

A shout echoed from the RV. Simon's blood raced as he got within a hundred yards. He looked around the campsite, his brain screaming at him to react. The minivan was positioned between him and the RV. Although the creatures had breached the RV, they'd left the minivan alone.

He sprinted toward the minivan, certain that the creatures would turn toward him in a single mass, but they remained preoccupied with the RV. Once they saw him, they'd charge. He just hoped for a few moments of reprieve—enough to get to the vehicle. He slipped through the trees as his arm pulsed pain, begging him to slow down. But he didn't. And then he was at the van, opening the door, hopping in.

One of the rifles was sitting in the passenger's seat. The other weapons were gone. Sandy must've grabbed what she could. At least, that was his guess. He recalled the pistol that had skittered under the RV, but that wouldn't help him now.

　　　　　　　　　　　　T.W. Piperbrook

Simon grabbed the rifle, stuck it on his lap, and started the van.

A handful of creatures turned in his direction.

Simon stomped the gas, steered toward the RV, stuck his rifle out the window, and fired. One of the creatures fell from the gunshot, while another hit the bumper of the minivan, tumbling sideways. Simon took a wide berth as he drove past the RV, keeping to the fringes of the hungry fray and driving over an open patch of forest. Rocks rumbled under the tires as he traveled over hard terrain. He shot several more creatures, balancing the wheel, knowing that if he stopped moving, he'd die.

He swerved past the RV and into the woods, narrowly avoiding a cluster of trees, and turned so he could spin around for another pass. Several of the creatures broke from the RV and ran, catching up. Simon hit the gas and raced forward, nicking the side of a tree with the front bumper.

He laid on the horn.

The noise was loud and piercing, overshadowing the hungry din of the creatures.

More of them broke from what they were doing and started following him. He let go of the horn and shot a few that were in proximity of the driver's side, sending them sprawling. Catching a glimpse through the RV's windshield, he saw movement inside.

"Sandy! Hector! Marcia!" he cried.

He gritted his teeth and rammed into several

other creatures as he swung back onto the dirt road. The minivan groaned in protest. Facing the RV, he watched as more creatures flooded toward him. He hit the horn several more times to keep their attention. Simon sped forward again, calling his companions' names. He heard a screamed response from inside the RV.

Someone was alive.

Using that noise to drive him, he fired his rifle out the window, drawing the attention of more creatures as he spun the wheel to turn around. The creatures gave chase, their eyes black and their expressions hungry. Simon headed for the dirt road, hoping he could lead them away.

43

"WHERE'S HE GOING?" HECTOR ASKED, looking out the windows as the minivan sped off.

Sandy's shock at seeing Simon alive was overshadowed by the fact that he was in danger. More of the creatures flooded from the RV to the minivan, following the moving target. Hector stabbed a few who were still trying to climb in the sills. Sandy slipped her blade into several of the creatures that had come in through the front windshield. Soon, nothing was left moving.

Bodies of the dead were sprawled over the seats and on the floor. Blood oozed into the seats. The odor of death filled the air. But the creatures were gone.

She looked back at Hector and Marcia. "We're not safe here," she warned, cleaning her knife on the floor.

"We need to leave," Hector agreed. "Is everyone okay?"

Marcia nodded. Her face was cut in several places, and her hair hung unevenly in spots where some of it had been ripped out. Hector had similar cuts and scrapes, but he seemed intact. They walked through the RV to retrieve Anabel. When they opened the bathroom door, Anabel leapt for her mother, holding Marcia tightly. Sandy felt a surge of warmth at seeing the girl unharmed.

"Simon will be back," Sandy said aloud, not wanting to consider the alternative.

"Where can we go that he'll find us?" Marcia asked.

Sandy thought about what Donna had told them. There was a chance they'd find other buildings, but they'd have to roam farther. She hadn't seen anything when they'd pulled into the campground.

"We've probably stirred up every creature for miles. Even if we found another place, Simon might miss us. I'm not sure where we should go," Hector said.

Sandy bit her lip, frustrated. She looked out the windows, but saw nowhere else they could hide.

Then she looked up.

They waited on the roof for an hour for Simon. During that time, the sun beat through the trees overhead and the crows circled, probably waiting for a crack at the dead creatures below. Before climbing up onto the RV's roof, they'd pulled Donna's body into an area of shade. It was the best they could do at that moment.

A few times, meandering creatures stalked

through the trees, searching for them. One actually came close enough to poke through the remains of its brethren. Each time Sandy, Hector, Marcia, and Anabel ducked flat, keeping unnoticed. Although the noise had drawn more creatures, the lack of recent gunshots seemed to have worked in their favor.

Sandy knew their luck wouldn't last.

Watching one of the creatures wander out of earshot, Sandy said, "I wonder if they remember what they were."

"If they do, they must be horrified at what their lives have become," Hector said.

Sandy's thoughts returned to Simon. It'd been a long time since she'd heard the sounds of the minivan. Long enough that she didn't want to think about what might've happened to him.

"How long should we wait?" Hector asked, voicing the unspoken question.

Sandy sighed nervously. "I'm not sure. Even if we wanted to leave, we have no way of getting out of here, except on foot."

She wanted to believe that Simon had survived, but the more time that passed, the greater her doubts grew. He'd effectively led the creatures away. He'd saved them. But what if he'd died? She swallowed as she thought back to what Simon had said at the elementary school.

Nobody else should have to die like Finn.

She prayed those words weren't a premonition. A day ago, she never would've believed that

Simon would be concerned about their welfare, but he'd proved to be a trusted ally since they'd left the lumberyard. He'd saved Hector and his family. He'd helped them all. She thought back to the conversation she'd shared with him in the utility shed, and the expression of sympathy he'd shown her.

Please let him be alive.

The purr of an engine interrupted her doomed thinking.

"Do you hear that?" Hector asked.

"Yes," Sandy said, sitting up.

They stared into the distance, watching a vehicle approach. The trees masked its shape, but it looked to be the same color as the minivan. It wasn't until she saw Simon driving that Sandy scrambled to her feet, waving. The van raced around the corner and pulled from the gravel onto the dirt road by the RV. The exterior was dented and stained. The driver's window was smashed. Simon looked up at them, attempting a smile before he slumped over against the steering wheel.

44

"JESUS CRISTO!" HECTOR EXCLAIMED AS they scrambled down the ladder of the RV.

Sandy reached Simon first. His hands were still on the wheel. He'd managed to put the minivan in park before falling over, but she saw a serious injury on his arm that looked like it'd been wrapped up with a piece of t-shirt. His face was cut and bleeding. His clothing was ripped. On his lap was the rifle she hadn't been able to carry from the minivan. Creatures' remains were spackled to the side of it.

"Simon!" she hissed, frantic that he might've died.

Simon's eyes were half-closed. She tried leaning him back in the seat and talking to him, but he barely responded. Without wanting to, Sandy recalled Harold. Maybe Simon had lost too much blood already.

"I'll get the medical supplies!" Marcia cried, racing to the back of the minivan.

"And some water!" Sandy called after her.

Hector and Sandy tried to revive the wounded man, with little result.

"Simon, can you hear us?" Sandy asked, peering in at the man.

He groaned.

"Thank God. He's alive. Everything's going to be all right, okay?" Sandy said.

He opened his eyes slightly and nodded. He seemed lucid, but exhausted.

Taking the water from Marcia, Sandy gently undid the piece of t-shirt with which he'd wrapped his injury. Underneath was a bloody stab wound.

"Is this from Reginald?" Sandy surmised.

Simon nodded.

"Is he dead?"

Another nod.

"Help me hold him up, Hector," Sandy requested. There was no time to think about the events that had transpired. Right now she needed to help her friend.

Hector assisted while they gently sat Simon upright and addressed the wound.

"Marcia, would you mind keeping watch for us?"

Marcia nodded and aimed her pistol over the forest. Sandy used water and gauze to clean the wound, then re-bandaged it the best she could. The injury looked painful, but it seemed like he could move his arm. That was a good sign.

In an ideal world, Simon would need stitches, but they didn't have the supplies to do any more that what she did.

"We should go," Hector said nervously, looking around.

"Let's get him in the back seat," Sandy said.

"We're going to help you out of the van, okay, Simon?"

"Okay," he croaked.

Hector, Marcia, and Sandy lifted Simon from the front seat, tucking their hands underneath his armpits. They brought him around to the back seat. He walked unsteadily, but made the transition. When they had him inside, Sandy took the driver's seat while Hector rode next to her. Marcia and Anabel stayed in the back with Simon.

The forest around them had succumbed to silence. Sandy felt a wave of uneasy déjà vu. She surveyed the scattered bodies of the dead that covered the ground and the bloodied hood of the RV. Somewhere in the woods lay Donna's body. They wouldn't have time to bury her, just like they hadn't had the chance to bury Finn.

As if sensing thoughts, Hector said, "Let's get as far away from this area as we can."

Sandy couldn't stop checking the rearview mirror as they left the campground. They saw no more creatures. Marcia tended Simon, managing to get him to swallow some water and pain medication. He mumbled his appreciation. Sandy knew the medication would take some time to kick in, and it wouldn't alleviate the discomfort of a stab wound, but she was grateful they had something.

Sandy watched the road around them, as if the

creatures might spring a coordinated attack, even though she hadn't seen any in a while. Simon must've taken care of most of the things in the area.

Simon said he'd killed Reginald.

Though she wasn't one to harbor vindictive thoughts, Sandy hoped Reginald was lying somewhere in a ditch, unable to harm them. He'd killed Charlie. He'd indirectly killed Donna. She hoped his reign of terror was done.

The ponderosa pines were thick with branches, making the area peaceful and serene. Sandy was more on edge than before, if that was possible. She was worried about Simon.

Looking at Simon's hunched figure in the backseat, she prayed he'd be all right.

"Where are we going?" Hector asked, pulling her from her thoughts.

"I'm not sure," she responded. "I didn't realize it at first, but I've been driving deeper into the mountains."

"Do you think the bunker is still the best plan?" Hector asked.

"I don't know," Sandy said with a sigh.

"I wish we could find help," Marcia said. "*Real* help."

They were surprised when Simon uttered something from the backseat. "Keep going."

He readjusted, pulling the map from his pocket. He passed it up to them. Hector turned in surprise, accepting it. "You need stitches. We need a doctor."

"I don't think we'll find one," Simon managed. "I'll survive. We'll figure it out when we get to the bunker."

Hector was quiet a moment. "But what if the bunker's not there? For all we know, we won't be able to follow these directions. Or maybe the place doesn't exist."

Hector was voicing everyone's worst fear.

"It's worth a try," Simon managed to say, before closing his eyes and slipping into whatever pain-induced haze he'd been in.

"How close are we to the bunker?" Marcia asked.

"About ten miles." Sandy blew a breath. She exchanged a look with Hector as they considered their options. "I think Simon's right. After what we've seen in the mountains, the bunker might be our only option."

45

HECTOR STUDIED THE MAP, TRYING to decipher it. "After the turnoff, the rest of the distance is on foot. It looks like this place is in the mountains."

"That's what Simon said."

Sandy's heart plummeted as she thought about the journey. Simon was weak and in pain. How could they expect him to make that journey? They'd have to figure it out when they got there.

She clamped her hands on the wheel as the road kept ascending, curving and twisting over mountain ranges, revealing a view that was both breathtaking and terrifying. Sandy had never been afraid of heights, but then again, she'd never faced heights such as these. She pictured the minivan tumbling off a turn and pitching them to a bloody death, where no one would find them. Who was left to look for them?

They drove the ten miles in relative silence, alternating between checking their surroundings and checking on Simon, making sure he was all right. Finally, they approached a brown, rectangular sign.

"That's it," Hector said, pointing to the side of the road.

Sandy studied the area. Unlike the campsite they'd stopped in before, this one had tents and cars. She knew it was normal for tourists to be in the mountains, but vehicles and shelters meant the infected.

She slowed to a crawl. Heat poured through the broken driver's side window. They'd cleaned some of the blood and fluid from the minivan's interior, but the smell still lingered, and there was still glass on the floor. Hector reached for the rifle on his lap, and Sandy gripped her pistol. They'd expended most of their ammunition in the RV battling the creatures.

The campground around them was quiet and still, as if it had been waiting for someone to appear. The cars were lifeless. Many of the doors were left open, as if the owners had stepped out and intended to return. The tents hung open, flapping in the soft breeze. A few of the sleeping bags contained moving bodies, but she knew better than to think the people weren't infected. The air smelled of death and decay, things rotting in the sweltering heat.

Sandy held her breath and kept driving.

Passing another tent, she saw one of the creatures moving erratically from wall to wall, pressing on the fabric, hissing. It looked like a small child; someone must've trapped it, rather than killing it. Sandy felt a wave of sadness.

They kept going, winding through the campground streets while Hector studied the directions, and the tents and cars grew farther and farther apart. Every so often, a body lay on the asphalt, half-eaten by rodents.

Soon they'd reached a narrow dirt road with only a few vacant tents. A station wagon sat idly, the back window smashed. Sandy had a brief thought of Dan and Quinn, but this vehicle was red instead of blue. She wondered if she'd ever see them again.

"I think this is where we're supposed to park," Hector noted.

"Okay. We walk now?" Sandy asked.

Hector nodded. They looked at the thick woods, trying to determine the danger lurking between the trees. But they'd never be rid of it. They'd have to forge ahead, just like they'd done since the start of the infection, just like they'd done since leaving the lumberyard. Sandy pulled into a spot away from the tents and station wagon.

To her surprise, Simon's eyes were open when she looked in the rearview.

"I'm not staying here, so don't even ask," he mumbled.

They walked through the forest in a tight group, helping Simon and carrying several bags of supplies. Sandy was reminded of the walk from the truck to the school, only this time, they moved much more slowly due to Simon's injury. Sandy understood why he'd insisted on coming.

After all they'd been through, was one place any safer than another?

She recalled the people in St. Matthews she'd seen running, driving, and hunkering down. Whether or not they got caught always depended on luck, or the will of God. She wasn't sure which.

Looking at Simon, noticing he seemed more lucid than he had an hour ago, she asked, "What happened to Reginald?"

A look crossed Simon's face as he gathered the strength to speak. "He got ahold of my knife, and he tried to kill me. I was barely able to fend him off."

He relayed the rest of his story, skipping some of the specifics. Sandy got the picture of how gruesome the battle had been. It didn't make her feel any sense of justice. She watched Simon as he spoke, still in disbelief that he'd survived.

"He would've killed me in those woods, the way he did Charlie, or Donna."

Sandy nodded. "Of course he would've. You did what you had to."

"What about the creatures that were chasing the van?" Marcia asked.

"I picked off as many as I could while I lured them away. I was so preoccupied that I hit a tree. They surrounded me. That's when they smashed the window. I shot as many as I could, but I ran out of ammunition. And then I used my knife. I can still feel them on me, their teeth clacking together while they tried to devour me alive. I'm still not sure how I got away."

Sandy watched his pained expression. It certainly explained his disheveled, ripped clothing. Hearing his story was enough to make her relive those moments of claustrophobia, when all she'd heard were the groans of the creatures in St. Matthews.

Once we get to the bunker, it'll all be worth it.

They snuck through the forest, supporting Simon while Hector traced the map. Using the sun as a guide, they tried to keep a consistent direction.

"We're looking for a hill that leads into a mountain. It should be close."

They passed several clusters of trees that Sandy swore she'd seen before, though she couldn't be sure. The landmarks all looked the same after a while. After a few miles, they found the hill that Hector had spoken about.

"That's it," he hissed. "That's the next thing on the map."

46

THEY HIKED WITH RENEWED VIGOR, helping Simon up the steep hill. The thick trees segued into a sparse overlook. Through a thick patch of foliage, Sandy saw a landscape of mountains and blue sky. Birds were circling and swooping, spotting things of interest and diving out of sight. Soon they were out of the foliage and walking up the thin ridge of a mountain.

Looking over the edge, Sandy felt the same vertigo she'd experienced while driving on the windy mountain roads, but this was worse. She steadied herself and tightened her stomach. Sandy forced herself to look away from the massive drop. They were deep in the White Mountains, far away from anyone who might be able to assist, even if times were normal. She clutched Simon's arm, helping him over a patch of rocks so he wouldn't slip, as he grunted in pain. She balanced her bag of food.

"Maybe I should've stayed in the van," he said with a grim smile.

"And miss this beautiful trip?" Sandy asked. "How could you?"

Simon grinned weakly. They measured their steps on the narrow path, forcing themselves to look straight ahead. The only navigable path snaked near the edge of a fall a hundred feet down. Roots and weeds jutted from every crevice where they were walking. The area was overgrown and treacherous. Had they not been following a map, they would never have followed it.

When she dared take a glance, Sandy saw mountains rising in every direction. The landscape was breathtaking, but dangerous enough that she couldn't allow herself to be distracted for too long.

Soon, they reached a flatter portion of the mountain, where the ridge became a flat, wide expanse of smooth rock. Looking behind her, Sandy saw that they were halfway around the mountain. The view was incredible. Thick mountain crags jutted out above and below them. Hector stopped, cupping his hand over his eyes as he read the map. He pointed to a distant valley.

"See that patch of land down there?" he asked, gesturing at the flowing green grass. "That's the end of the directions."

Sandy felt a surge of excitement. That excitement quickly turned into doubt. The land was wild and untouched, as if neither humans nor animals had ever set foot on it. She couldn't imagine anyone building anything out here.

She paused to catch her breath while Simon halted beside her. She looked out across the smooth rock landscape, wiping a stream of sweat from her brow.

"You're sure that's where the map ends?" she asked Hector.

He bit his lip. "Yep."

"I guess we have no choice but to go down and check it out."

They searched between the thick blades of grass in the valley for a door. Hector handed Sandy the map, but she was as puzzled by the scrawled notes as he was. The last few notes were unreadable. She saw nothing that looked man-made, buried or otherwise.

"I don't see how this can be it," she said.

Beyond the grassy plain was another rising mountain. Pointed crags warned of an equally dangerous journey. The day was getting late. If they'd been misled, or had taken a wrong turn, they'd have to consider the possibility of camping on the flat, grassy valley.

Sandy stared into the distance. On the other side of the valley, following the base of the next mountain, she noticed a long, narrow body of water.

"What's that?" he asked.

They hadn't noticed it at first, due to several large boulders along the edge. The brook was flowing behind them. The sight renewed her hope.

"It looks like a brook," Hector commented.

A body of water meant something to drink.

Sandy wasn't sure how clean the water would be, but it must be better than the contaminated liquid in town. She considered the bottles of clean water they had in the bags — bottles that could be refilled.

Maybe the hideaway had never been a hideaway at all.

Maybe the place was a shelter without walls.

The long grass tickled Sandy's ankles as they walked to the brook. The air smelled clean and pure. Sandy had a feeling of exhilarating freedom unlike any she'd had in a while. She knelt down next to the water. The others did the same. Sandy slipped her hands into the cold, surging brook, testing the current, letting the water flow past her hands. She set down her gun and bag of food. Next to her, Hector, Marcia, and Anabel did the same. For a moment, they were able to forget some of the horrors they'd lived through. Maybe this was the end of their journey.

Maybe this is what they were meant to find.

Sandy closed her eyes, absorbing that feeling of the cold water on her hands. When she opened them, she noticed a man tucked into the large outcropping of rock next to them. He held a gun as he peeked out from the crevices.

"Don't move," he said.

47

"**D**ON'T MOVE," THE MAN REPEATED.

Sandy, Simon, Hector, Marcia, and Anabel froze. Their hands were still dipped in the brook, their guns on the bank next to them. The man was twenty feet away. His face was flecked with stubble. A tan hunter's cap on his head covered sprouts of gray hair.

Sandy removed her hands to raise them.

"I said don't move!" the man yelled, forcing her to freeze.

His voice carried over the gentle rush of the water. The others held a tense silence as they waited for him to speak again. They'd been through enough to know that responding might lead to shooting.

"I knew someone would come," he said, regaining his calm as he held his position. "You must have my sons' map."

No one answered.

"You do," he guessed.

Receiving no response to his question, the man crept out from behind the rock, watching them intently. Sandy had the instinct to run, but she knew she'd never get far enough away to avoid a bullet.

"Did you kill them?" the man asked. "Did you kill my boys?"

Sandy's heart sank as she remembered the dead bodies of the men at the elementary school. She could still see their pale lips, their vacant eyes.

"They're dead, aren't they?" The man shook his gun and waited for an answer. This time, anger flashed in his face.

Hector spoke up quietly. "They tried to kill my family. We defended ourselves."

"My sons wouldn't harm anyone." The man shook his head.

Sandy recalled the looks of violence in the men's eyes as they'd stalked Hector and his family. Sandy didn't need to second-guess herself to know they were ill intentioned.

"Wait a minute," Hector said, recalling something. "The men who tried to kill us took the map from others. They forced someone to write the directions on it."

"What are you talking about?"

"They forced your boys to give it to them. I overheard them talking," Hector explained. He described the men they'd encountered.

"I know their names," Sandy interrupted. "Dwight Pickman and Samuel Black. Do those names sound familiar?"

"No." Anger and doubt crossed over the man's face. He sucked in deep, tense breaths as he surveyed them. He kept his aim on them. "Why should I believe you?"

"Check the handwriting on the map," Sandy said, nodding at Hector to give it to him. "Maybe it belongs to your boys."

Moving slowly, Hector recovered the map from his pocket and handed it to the man, who took it carefully and studied it.

After a moment, he shook his head. "This handwriting doesn't belong to either of my sons. For all I know, you wrote this."

"We defended ourselves from these other men. I'm not sure what else I can say to convince you," Hector said.

The man sighed and took a step back, surveying the mountains in the distance. For a moment, Sandy was certain he'd turn the gun back on them. Instead, he looked at them with sadness in his eyes. "I knew something went wrong when they didn't arrive. My sons should've been here days ago."

"They were going to meet you here?" Sandy guessed.

"That was my hope." The man spat on the ground. "My boys thought I was crazy, always preparing and talking about the end of the world. But I knew something would happen one day. I just wasn't sure what. I took them up here once. I gave them the map."

"I'm sorry," Sandy said, softly. "Are you up here alone?"

The man watched her for a moment, as if he still couldn't trust her. "I used to come up here with my wife, Martha. But she died a few years ago. Colon cancer."

"I'm sorry," Sandy said.

"She's probably better off, not having to live through this hell." The man looked away.

"There's a possibility your sons are still out there," Sandy said hopefully.

The man shook his head. "When this started, I went looking for them in town. I found their car a few streets from my house. It was full of blood. I never found the bodies."

"You've been keeping watch, waiting for them," Sandy guessed.

The man nodded. "I kept telling myself they were coming. Maybe I was foolish. When I saw you coming down the mountain, I assumed you killed them."

Sandy felt a wave of sadness for the man. It seemed like he'd lost as much as the rest of them. She was surprised when he chuckled.

"What is it?" she asked.

"Even though they were in danger, my boys must've remembered what I taught them."

"What do you mean?"

"My boys gave those men the wrong directions."

Hector looked around the field, confused. "So there's no shelter here?"

"Not in the valley," the man replied with a sad smile as he cranked a thumb over his shoulder at the incline. "My shelter's on the mountain."

48

"MY NAME'S CARTER," THE MAN said as he led them across a shallow part of the brook, where stones and sticks made a natural pathway across the water. Sandy introduced herself and the others.

"I appreciate you helping us," said Sandy, following closely behind him. "I appreciate you trusting us."

"I have an intuition about people," Carter said. "If you had lied about the map, I might've shot you," he admitted.

As they walked, Sandy relayed the story they'd heard from Dan about the contamination.

"I always knew this would happen. This, or something like it." Carter looked into the distance. "Things are bad out there. The world seems to be getting worse—terrorism, shootings, and murders every time you turn around. No one has any respect for each other anymore. The world is a lawless place. I figured it was only a matter of time until society disintegrated."

Carter led them around the base of a mountain, keeping the brook in view until they ascended a heavy incline. They trekked through mountain trails that seemed untouched by the hands of man, gaining a view even more spectacular than the one they'd seen before. Sandy wondered if anyone besides Carter had been up here in many years. She doubted it.

They followed the curve of a mountain, passing several deep openings underneath the crags of the cliff. She was surprised when Carter disappeared underneath one of them.

"Under here," he called over his shoulder.

She and the others ducked down, following him into a small opening in the mountainside that would've been imperceptible to someone who wasn't looking for it. Soon they were standing upright, and Carter was leading them through a manmade door that was barely visible in the shadows. The door opened into a room about twenty feet wide and twenty feet long—large enough to accommodate all of them. Carter lit several lanterns, which looked like they were solar-powered. Canned goods were stacked on shelves next to the walls. Everywhere she looked, Sandy saw supplies: fishing lures, rods, sleeping bags, medical supplies. Through a smaller, carved out door, she saw a room with a cot and several camping chairs.

"It took me years of preparation to build this," Carter said, answering her unspoken question. "I have enough supplies here to last for many years."

Sandy marveled at the supply of canned goods, the quantity of which she might've expected to find in a basement, not in a room on some deserted mountain.

"And you built this by yourself?" Simon asked.

"It took a lot of probing, and some digging." Carter smiled. "And a lot of research. The closest you can get to this place by car is a few miles. Martha helped me pick the spot. She used to humor me, before she died. I'm not sure she ever believed me, fully, but she was a good woman."

Clearing his throat, Carter walked to one of the shelves and brought out a medical kit. He beckoned to Simon. "Let me have a look at that wound. I can probably stitch you up."

Simon unwrapped the makeshift bandage. "I was stabbed by a man that was trying to kill us," he explained. "We've run into some bad luck, as you can imagine."

"I believe it." Carter pulled out one of the camping stools so Simon could sit. He inspected the wound. "I used to be a paramedic in my younger years."

Simon nodded.

"You'll probably want some of this, first," Carter said, retrieving a bottle of bourbon from a shelf.

"Thanks," Simon said, taking the bottle and swigging off it.

While Carter prepared to stitch up Simon, Hector asked, "You said you were a paramedic?"

"Yes, in my twenties," Carter said. "For most of my life, I was a history professor."

Sandy looked at him, surprised. "A history professor?"

"I retired a few years ago. Studying history is what prompted me to build all this," Carter explained. "I've seen what humanity does to itself over the years. I've seen the cycles of violence repeated over the years. The world has become too self-absorbed. Technology hasn't helped us any, in that regard. I knew it was only a matter of time until society collapsed. That's when I began searching for a place like this. About five years ago, I found it, and I started building. It's a work in progress."

Having prepared for giving stitches, Carter went to work with practiced hands. Simon flinched several times, but did his best to keep a brave face.

"Do you think the agents are really behind this?"

Carter nodded knowingly. "Yes. In fact, nothing you told me is a surprise."

"What do you mean?" Sandy asked.

"I've been listening to transmissions, piecing things together since I've been up here." Carter took a breath. "I have a shelf full of radios in the other room. The people you're speaking about have been planning this for years. They've been waiting for this moment, and for a perfect first target. St. Matthews was ground zero for the contamination."

49

"OW CAN YOU KNOW THAT?" Hector asked, an expression of shock on his face.

"There's a network out there, Hector, people like me who are hunkered down and listening to things. St. Matthews was the first target for these men. They used it as a test run so they could infect other areas. Their goal was to get rid of enough of us to cause a collapse, so they could take over and build a new civilization."

Sandy digested the information. "Unbelievable. How far has this spread?"

"Texas, Oklahoma, Colorado, New Mexico, and Arizona. But it seems to have been contained now."

"By the government?"

"No." Carter grinned. "By civilians. A few days ago, some people located the compound housing the agents and killed many of them. I don't know all the details, but that's what I heard from some of my transmissions."

"That must mean the army is out there," Sandy asked, hope blossoming inside her.

"Yes. According to what I heard, the military is setting up a compound in St. Matthews, among other places. They were headed here from the White Sands Missile Range in New Mexico."

"Did they arrive?"

"I'm not sure. That was the last I heard," Carter admitted. "The radios have been fairly quiet."

Sandy shook her head incredulously.

"If there is a compound in St. Matthews, then we can find help, real help," Sandy said, unable to contain her excitement. "Your sons might even be there."

Carter shook his head. "I know better than to believe that."

"Don't you want to find out for sure?"

Carter watched them silently for a moment. "I might be a foolish old man, but I have no desire to go back to St. Matthews. Not now, not ever."

"What are you going to do?" Hector asked. "Stay up here forever?"

"Why not?" Carter shrugged, pointing to a bow on the wall. "I can hunt. I can fish. I have water from the brook to boil and drink. I have plenty of supplies. I've been preparing for something like this for most of my life. I'll get by, like I always do."

"Won't it be dangerous living out here? You'll have no way to get help quickly, if something should happen," Sandy said.

"No more dangerous than living out there."

Sandy frowned. She wasn't ready to accept his answer. "Your sons might be looking for you.

I know you think they're dead, but you have to have hope."

"If, by the grace of God, my sons survived, they'll know where to look for me. Otherwise, I have no reason to go back."

Sandy blew a sad breath, but she understood the man's reasoning. Still, she felt a strong urge to get to the compound.

"We should leave now," Sandy said. "We shouldn't waste any more time. If they're really setting up a compound in St. Matthews, it's in our best interest to get there."

"I wouldn't suggest leaving now, unless you want to go through the mountains in the dark. Those creatures are everywhere, and traveling with flashlights isn't a smart move. It'll be dusk soon. I'd suggest leaving in the morning."

"He's probably right," Simon agreed.

"Get some rest," Carter said. "I'll cook you some dinner. Afterward, I'll see if I can get more concrete information."

"I don't know how to thank you," Sandy said.

"Don't," Carter said. "The only thing I ask is that you tell no one about where I'm staying. I don't want anyone else showing up here. I've trusted you. I've brought you in. Don't make me regret it."

Sandy and the others nodded. They wouldn't break their promise. Sandy closed her eyes and reopened them. She was still in disbelief of what she'd heard. For the first time since the contamination started, she felt a sense of real hope — a hope that was calling to her from beyond the shelter door.

Carter took out a small burner and a pot, opened a can of beans, and put them over the flame. They watched quietly as Carter cooked and dished out portions of beans for them.

"I don't understand how these people could get away with this," Hector said. "It seems insane."

Carter didn't seem as shocked as them. "We are the most advanced we've ever been, but at the same time, we're the most vulnerable. The whole world is interconnected. That leads to a lot of great possibilities, but also some horrific ones."

Sandy told them how her credit card information had once been stolen. "Nothing is truly safe, is it?"

"The government can't regulate all the technology we're developing. And they certainly can't keep watch over everyone. I'm sure there are a lot of people who want this to happen, people who desire it badly enough that they'd find a way to coordinate it, no matter how much time or money it takes."

"Do you think the government knew about any of this?" Sandy asked.

"Who knows?" Carter shrugged. "My guess is that they didn't know what was happening until it had already been done. All they can do now is clean up the aftermath."

"I hope it's really over," Marcia said, biting her lip.

"There's no way to know for sure," Carter said.

They finished eating, assisting Carter in cleaning up the dishes. Sandy was surprised to find that her stomach was sated by the meal. Perhaps it was the knowledge that, for the moment, they were safe, and that the possibility of rescue — real rescue — was close. She smiled at Simon as he put away some of Carter's supplies. He seemed to be doing better than he had been before. For a moment, Sandy almost convinced herself she was a guest in someone's home, and that soon they'd say their goodbyes, heading home to the same apartments and houses they'd left. It was hard to believe that those places were probably ravaged.

They grew quiet as they contemplated their journey in the morning. Carter pointed out several places where they could sleep, offering them sleeping bags and blankets.

"These were going to be for my wife and sons. At least someone will use them." His sad smile seemed genuine. "I'm going to listen to some broadcasts while you rest. See if I can find some confirmation that the compound is being set up."

"Thanks, Carter," Sandy said, and she meant it.

"I'm sure you're tired, but before you get some sleep, you should see the view," Carter said with a knowing smile.

"What do you mean?" Sandy asked.

"We're pretty high up. You won't believe what you can see from here."

The sun had just started descending beyond the distant mountains, casting an amber orange glow in the sky. Lingering beams of light illuminated the hills and peaks over which they'd traveled.

"Carter was right. It's beautiful," Sandy said to the others.

Simon, Hector, Marcia, and Anabel agreed.

They watched the sun sink lower and darkness creep in, each of them quiet and reflective. After a while, Hector and his family went inside to clean up and get ready for bed while Sandy remained outside with Simon. They stood in silence for a while.

"When I was in that minivan, watching the creatures coming at me, I thought I was dead," Simon said to Sandy. "I never thought I'd be standing here right now."

Sandy smiled. In truth, she'd harbored some of those same thoughts, though she'd prayed he'd be all right. "Every morning I wake up, I wonder what horror the next day will bring. But for the first time in a while, I'm looking forward to tomorrow."

"Do you think we'll reach the compound?" Simon asked.

"I don't see why not," Sandy said. "We've gotten through everything else. Hopefully it exists, though I get nervous about Carter's warnings. Do you think something like this will happen again?"

Simon sighed. "I think Carter's right to be cautious. But I have a good feeling about this compound. For the first time in a while, I have a feeling we're going to be all right."

"I want to believe that."

"Then do it."

Simon reached over and found her hand. She squeezed him back. They stood next to each other in a comfortable silence for several more minutes, taking in the stars and the hoots of night animals, and then retired to the bunker to get some sleep.

50

THEY PACKED THEIR BELONGINGS AT first light. Overnight, Carter had gotten an approximate location of where the compound was located, though he couldn't say for sure whether it was still there.

"The radios were quiet all night," he said. "I'm not sure what's happening. Are you sure you want to leave?"

Sandy looked at the others briefly before nodding. "Yes. We have to try. If things don't go as planned, we can always come back, right?"

"Of course."

Carter sent them with additional food to complement the supplies they had, as well as a compass. He gave them explicit instructions on how to reach the campsite, though they'd traveled that way the day before. Even though he'd known them a short time, he seemed worried about them. When they'd exhausted the last of their plans, they headed for the door.

"Thanks for everything, Carter," Sandy told him.

"Don't mention it," he said as he led them to the door. He lingered, watching them with a look of nostalgia. Maybe he was thinking about his sons.

"Are you sure you're not coming?" Sandy looked at him, hoping he might change his mind.

Carter remained steadfast. "I'm sure. If you find my sons, please tell them I'm alive. They'll know where to find me."

They nodded, saying farewell. And then he was opening the door for them, and they were traveling the same path they'd come the day before. Sandy glanced over her shoulder several times as they walked down the steep, narrow mountain, giving Carter a wave as they descended.

And then he was out of sight.

She wondered what the coming days would bring for him, what his life would be like. A part of her couldn't imagine living in the secluded hideaway alone, with only the mountains and the distant valleys and forest for company. Another part of her decided it might be liberating.

She wished nothing but the best for him.

The trip went faster than the day before. With a night's rest under their belts, and Simon stitched up, they were able to pick up the pace. They hiked the same valley and mountain path they'd taken the day before, recognizing several landmarks. Even Anabel kept up with the grownups, her small legs pumping as she hiked.

"Are we going home now?" she asked Hector and Marcia.

"I'm not sure, honey," Hector said. "But we'll see."

Sandy had barely blinked before several hours had passed. They traveled over the hill and through the thick forest, approaching the campground. The minivan was in the same place in which they had left it. Two creatures hovered around the vehicle, staring through the open driver's side window. Their hisses carried over the wind. It had been long enough since they'd seen one of the creatures that Sandy had almost convinced herself they weren't real.

They disposed of the things with knives to the head, and then packed their belongings inside. Other than a thin layer of pine needles stuck to the windshield, the vehicle was untouched. They got inside with haste and assumed the positions that had become routine, by now.

"Are you sure you're up for driving?" Hector asked Sandy.

"Yes," she said, "I want to."

She looked in the backseat. Marcia and Anabel gave her frightened but hopeful smiles. Simon gave her a confident nod.

She started the car. Several creatures lurked through the campsite as they drove through it, staring at the vehicle.

"Is it just me, or are they moving slower than before?" Sandy asked.

Hector watched them with a curious expression on his face. "Maybe they're tired. Maybe they've had enough."

"I think we all have," Simon agreed.

51

HE JOURNEY DOWN THE MOUNTAIN was uneventful. They passed several abandoned, wrecked vehicles, but the turnoffs to the campsites looked just as deserted as when they'd passed them on the way up. Sandy's foot began to tire from driving. She felt as if she were constantly hitting the brakes, descending down a mountain that was treacherous to climb, and was no less treacherous to descend. She kept away from the edge and steered with caution.

Soon they were rolling into town. Sandy kept her eyes on the lifeless streets. Her hope was that they'd see a cavalry of military and police officers, waiting for them, but the town was as empty as before. The wind gusted, carrying several papers over the hood of the minivan. One of them stuck to the grille, flapping and unsticking.

"What if something happened, and no one's here?" she asked.

The others watched the road in silence, hit with the first moment of despair since leaving.

"We need to get across town," Hector said, pointing at one of the turns. "That's the only way we'll know for sure."

Sandy took the turns with a practiced ease,

driving around wrecked vehicles and rubbish that would've been out of place just a while ago, but was commonplace now. They drove through some of the same streets they'd traveled before, heading to the other side of town, keeping away from the main roads. Soon they were approaching the street to which Carter had directed them.

Gunshots pierced the air.

Sandy stiffened and clutched the wheel.

"What was that?" Marcia whispered from the backseat.

She slowed the vehicle to a crawl as she tried to determine the source of the noise. In the backseat, Simon, Marcia, and Anabel strained to get a better view.

They scrutinized the area, looking past industrial buildings that had sprung up on either side of the road. Cars turned at various angles blocked their view of the roadway. The noise seemed to be coming from a few streets away.

"The commotion is coming from where we're headed," Hector said nervously. "Should we turn around?"

A spike of fear coursed through Sandy at the thought of coming across more violent, crazed individuals.

"Wait. I see something," Hector said, peering out the windshield.

Suddenly, Anabel spoke up. "Army people!"

Several men in army fatigues came into view as they rounded a bend, pointing guns at creatures in the road, shooting them down. As they curved with the road, Sandy saw a line of military Humvees and jeeps parked across the street—a glimmer of order in an otherwise chaotic landscape. Groups of men with masks uncurled a fence, staking it off in the ground. Behind them, a few more were setting up tents. The men in fatigues looked up, noticing the minivan.

"My God," Marcia said as she hugged Anabel. "Carter was right."

"Put your guns on the floor," Hector said as he looked at the others. "We don't want them to think we're dangerous."

Sandy pulled up, stopping several hundred feet away from the soldiers. She let the vehicle idle as several soldiers cautiously approached them. Men wearing masks came up to the driver's side, instructing Sandy and the others to put her hands in the air. They complied without argument. Sandy watched the approaching soldiers in disbelief, still shocked to see them, still shocked that it wasn't a dream.

One of the soldiers took the lead. His hair was dark underneath his military cap.

"Are you armed?" he called in.

"Our weapons are on the floor."

"We'll need you to leave them where they are."

"Of course." Sandy swallowed, caught between nervousness and relief.

"Are any of you infected?" he asked, as several people in white Hazmat suits approached the vehicle.

"No," Sandy said, realizing how lucky she was to speak those words.

"We'll need to check you out."

"Of course. I can't believe you're here."

"You're the first survivors we've found alive in St. Matthews. I'm Sgt. Hicks."

Gunfire rattled in the background as Sgt. Hicks led them to a medical tent that was just being set up. They watched as a bustle of military, CDC, and other teams established fences outside the perimeter, while others warded off the roaming infected.

"You'll need to be tested for signs of the infection," Sgt. Hicks explained, as they waited for the team to get supplies in place. "We need to make sure you aren't a danger to anyone."

"I understand," Sandy said.

Hicks cleared his throat as he prepared more instructions. "You'll spend a few hours in medical, being tested and observed. When you're finished and cleared, we'll take statements." He paused, his demeanor turning from stern to compassionate.

T.W. Piperbrook

"I know you've been through a lot. Frankly, we could use all the information we can get."

Sandy and her companions followed Hicks to a medical tent, where they were tested and observed. The examinations felt like they went on forever — pokes, prods and blood tests, questions that Sandy felt like she answered several times. But she understood the precaution. Being tested was better than the alternative: being left to deal with the creatures in a violent, unpredictable world. She was glad they'd gotten to safety.

When they'd finished, Hicks brought them to a long, white trailer. Sandy waited her turn while Simon went first. A military woman with the name badge "Johnson" was ordered to stand guard next to them while the fences were still being finished.

Turning to Hector, Sandy said, "I never thought I'd see this much order again."

"It's unbelievable," Hector marveled.

The gunfire had died down, but the soldiers had taken to walking the perimeter, surveying the mountains and the roads. Others unfolded tents, setting them up with ease. In one tent, Sandy saw people unpacking what looked like cooking supplies. She hadn't eaten much since leaving Carter's. They'd only had a light breakfast. Her stomach grumbled at the thought of food.

"We'll get you something to eat soon," said Johnson, determining the reason behind Sandy's gaze. Johnson's smile was stoic, but warm.

Before Sandy could answer, the trailer door opened and Simon came out, watching her.

"Your turn," he told Sandy.

52

T HE TRAILER WAS AS CLEAN and organized as the rest of camp. Several shelves full of files and computers lined one wall. The floor was immaculate. Hicks and another man with white hair sat in chairs opposite Sandy, taking notes as they questioned her.

The men exchanged a glance before asking, "If you wouldn't mind, we'd like you to tell the story of how you ended up here."

Sandy launched into her tale without hesitation, telling of how she'd discovered her brother, how she'd hid out in St. Matthews, and how they'd escaped the lumberyard. She said that they'd begun searching for help in the mountains, but had returned when they hadn't found help. She made sure to give them information on Dan and Quinn, but she left out anything about Carter.

"You're lucky to be alive," Hicks told her. His expression seemed genuine.

"How long will we be staying here?" Sandy asked.

"We're not sure yet," the second man admitted. "We're in the beginning stages of knowing the scope of this thing. But your information will be helpful as we try to find others."

"I hope there are others to find," Sandy said.

"We've had some encouraging reports from some of the other camps," Hicks told her. "I have faith."

Sandy stood next to Simon as they looked over the newly constructed fences and tents, marveling at how empty they looked. In the coming days, those tents would fill with people, if Hicks were to be believed.

"There are bound to be other people who were immune," Simon said, watching the campsite.

"I hope so."

Behind them, Hector, Marcia, and Anabel hugged each other, grateful to be alive and safe. Sandy waited until Johnson had roamed farther away before she said anything else.

"What did you tell them?" Sandy asked, looking sideways at the trailer where they'd been questioned.

"The truth, for the most part," Simon said.

"Did you say anything about Carter?" Sandy asked.

"No." Simon shook his head, a smile crossing his face. "I wouldn't break that promise. The others won't, either."

"Good," Sandy said. She smiled and looked up at the mountains, picturing Carter sitting on some distant perch, watching them. She hoped he found peace, whether or not he found his sons. "We owe him for helping us."

She switched her focus to the soldiers milling around the campsite, some of who had finished setting up tents. She wondered which ones would house them. Would they have their own? Sandy couldn't imagine having a living space that she didn't share. Even at the lumberyard, she'd been lucky to get a spot to sleep on that wasn't right next to the others, with the constant need to keep guard over one another.

Her thoughts were interrupted by the sound of a car rolling up to the gate. Some of the soldiers stiffened. They made for the entrance, guns drawn as a brown sedan with scrapes and dents came to a slow stop in front of the compound.

"Who's that?" Simon asked, frowning.

"I'm not sure." Sandy shared his expression as they jogged toward the gate.

As they got closer, she half-hoped she'd find someone she recognized, but she'd never seen the people before. A man with a beard was hugging what appeared to be his wife. The survivors talked excitedly, pointing at the campground with the same look of hope that Sandy had probably just a few hours ago. The men in Hazmat suits led them from the vehicle, taking the same precautions they'd taken with Sandy and her group. Sandy bit her lip as she watched them.

"What were you thinking?" Simon asked.

"I was just thinking it might be Dan and Quinn," Sandy admitted. "Or Carter's sons."

"Me, too," Simon said.

They watched the newcomers talk animatedly for several minutes as the gates were opened and they were led inside. More men in protective suits surrounded them, ushering them toward the medical trailer.

"Dan and Quinn were heading over the mountains, right?" Simon asked.

"Yes. That was what they said. I was hoping we'd run into them while we were up there."

Simon stared down the road as he reflected on it. "You remember what I said about finding the compound?"

"Of course. You said you had a good feeling about it."

"Well, I have a good feeling about Dan and Quinn, too."

Sandy smiled. "You know what? So do I."

She let her smile linger as she took Simon's arm, leading him back toward the tents, where the smell of fresh cooked food drifted over the campsite.

THE END

AFTERWORD

Thanks for checking out Contamination 7! I hope you enjoyed Sandy's story. Although she started out as a minor character, I had a blast getting into her head and discovering what happened to her. Simon's character surprised me, too. I had a blast writing from his perspective. I hope you enjoyed reading the story as much as I enjoyed telling it.

What's next? If you haven't checked out Contamination: Dead Instinct, you can get that book now. I've had some requests for a follow-up to that story, so you never know when that might appear.

Want more? Leave a review and let me know. Reviews are like report cards. I never know what grade I'm going to get, but I always hope for an "A".

Until next time,
Tyler Piperbrook
June 2016

ALSO AVAILABLE:

THE LAST COMMAND (BOOK 4)
THE LAST REFUGE (BOOK 5)
THE LAST CONQUEST (BOOK 6)

ABOUT THE AUTHOR

T.W. Piperbrook lives in Connecticut with his wife and his son. He is the author of the **OUTAGE** series, the **CONTAMINATION** series, and the co-author of **THE LAST SURVIVORS**. In a former life, the author spent time as a full-time touring musician, traveling across the US, Canada, and Europe.

Now he spends his days fighting zombies, battling werewolves, and roaming Ancient cities.

Check out his website at: www.twpiperbrook.com

Edited by Cathy Moeschet
Proofread by Casey Skelton

Dedicated to my son Liam, who wanted to be included in the book (but I didn't have the heart to make him a zombie).

For more information on the author's work, visit: **http://www.facebook. com/twpiperbrook**